Hook, Line and Sinker

by

Martha Jane Shaw

Unintended Likenesses: This book is fiction. Any resemblance to real people, places, or things is unintended. The organizations and institutions referred to have not endorsed the opinions set forth by characters or actions in the book. Facts and figures in regard to Pacific bluefin tuna may vary but the rapid and urgent demise of this great species is, unfortunately, very true.

Contact: 617-921-9552
info@earthadvertising.com

Draft 4.0: 12/12/2016

Reviews

It's a really fun read, a gem of a book. I loved the real danger, revealing the real-world ruthlessness of the perpetrators. Natalie is a great character and an effective vehicle for understanding tuna and she hooks you into the mystery story. Another aspect of the book is the author's incredible descriptive narrative, politics and insider view of the graduate dilemma. It was perfect to see members of the graduate committee reacting to the data, and admiring her as a peer.

Dr. Susan Shaw
Marine Environmental Research Institute (MERI)

Was a fun read. We need more girl-power blue heroines like Natalie.

David Helvarg, Blue Frontier

I loved the concept and bones of the book. Being a single late 20s marine conservationist myself, it's relatable in some ways which aren't terribly common in books I have been reading lately.

Victoria Bell, Blue Frontier

So far, I like what I've seen.

Dr. Carl Safina, The Safina Center

Powerful, enlightening and entertaining with all the potential for a brilliant movie.

Frederick Johnston, Frederick Johnston

Martha Jane Shaw knocked it out the park with her first novel. I'm sharing it with everyone I know.

Doris Cadoux, Save our Oceans

I really enjoyed Hook, Line and Sinker, with its setting in La Jolla along with the SCUBA diving and adventures in oceanography I appreciate the homage that the writer paid to SIO Dive Locker supervisor Al Stover. I wonder where Natalie winds up next.

Mike Kirk, SIO Hydraulics Lab

To my family and friends, colleagues, oceanographers, teachers, fellows, readers of the book, to champions of the sea everywhere, and to the ocean we love.

Thanks to readers and listeners of the screenplay and the book including Diane Strack, Dr. Barbara Block, Doris Cadoux, Dr. Susan Shaw, Bonnie Blackwell, Victoria Bell, Martha Otis, Dr. Amanda Nickson, David Helvarg, Dr. Carl Safina, Dr. Sylvia Earle Leila Hadley Luce, Debbie Moore, TEC, Debbie Kinder, Jenifer Austin, Mike Kirk, Tessa Devonald, Patti Judd, Frederick Johnston, Rosalinda, Mariel Shaw, Joan Quinn Eastman, Richard Arroyo, and many others including Charlotte, Hazel, Francesca, Gaelin, Charlie, Spahr, Kaki, Hal, Paul, Patty, Milbry, Pew, Jan, Anne, Judy, Laura and others.

MJS

In memory of Dr. Kim Devonald

Forward

The story begins just after midnight in a marine biology laboratory at the Ocean Center in La Jolla, California, which is chiseled into the sedimentary cliffs that tower above the surf on Black's Beach.

Here, some of the world's most renowned oceanographers brainstorm with grad students to unravel the mysteries of the sea. The Center is over 100 years old, its halls a breeding ground for scientific discovery. When they awarded a PhD at the most reputable oceanographic think tank on earth, they made darn sure it meant something. The integrity of a degree from the Ocean Center could not be undermined.

Fictional character and doctoral candidate Natalie Scott had been studying Pacific bluefin tuna and their relatives in the Atlantic for nearly eight years. It was the bright, young grad student's task to characterize the present and predict the future of this marvelous marine creature.

6

Bluefin had been under siege since the 1970s when skyrocketing sushi markets made them a prize delicacy of the most expensive restaurants in the world. Meanwhile, superstores were selling cheap shrink-wrapped sashimi with a side of wasabi and soy sauce. Advertisements were lauding their lacerated corpses as brain food.

Before the sushi craze, people weren't much interested in feeding on the raw meat of the ocean's most magnificent warm-blooded fish who had roamed freely for over 50 million years according to geologic records. They weren't on the menu. Early man had adorned cave walls with elaborate drawings of bluefin along with other deities that they appeared to worship. Now, some people were willing to pay just about anything to eat them. In 2012 in Tsukiji, Japan, a single bluefin sold for $736,000. In 2013, one sold for $1.76 million.

If any creature could beat the odds against new sophisticated fishing technology and the greed of mankind, it could be them. These extreme human-sized athletes can swim fast like torpedoes across vast oceans and can dive 4000 feet.

They have powerful tails, retractable fins and extraordinary vision, though their eyes lay flush to their streamlined form. They can regulate their own temperature and easily swim from California coasts to mid-ocean seamounts to the breeding grounds in the Sea of Japan, and south to Australia, to Mexico and back. Long out-surviving dinosaurs, bluefin had seen just about everything. They had adapted for survival since the Paleocene era as the earth passed in and out of ice ages.

Larger-sized Atlantic bluefin had just narrowly escaped extinction just recently thanks to hard-fought regulations. The catch of their smaller Pacific cousins had yet to be adequately managed, leaving Pacific bluefin tuna poised to be next in line for the chopping block. It was grim. Even with regulations, many countries adhere and the rest do not. Double-blind private operations were ruled by profits and the high seas were subject to piracy as never before. To many, these natural marvels were no more than currency, and the ocean a treasure trove for the taking.

The Pacific bluefin population had quickly plummeted more than 96% in only half a century, leaving less than 4% of them left trying to stay alive. Most of the sashimi eaten were baby bluefin – juveniles less than five years old who had yet to spawn. One mother bluefin can spawn a million eggs at once making her a fertile species, which gives hope for a comeback. But not when all the babies are caught. Few lived to their expectancy of 15-26 years old. Many were simply ground up for fertilizer. Others rotted and were dumped at sea.

But still, yes there was hope. This sense of urgency, and Natalie's rapidly approaching deadline to finish her thesis, kept her up at night.

Natalie had been extrapolating numbers from data of all kinds that she was collecting from fish tagging and tracking programs, satellites, sensors, sushi and sashimi sales, canneries, restaurants, distributors, grocery chains, seafood markets, frozen food brands, pet food manufacturers, fertilizers, pharmaceuticals, sport fishing surveys, commercial catch numbers, juveniles illegally kidnapped for breeding, government contractor statistics, and from other less reliable sources. By factoring in migratory habits, ocean currents, population dynamics, feeding patterns, with breeding and mortality rates, she had hoped to publish the quintessential science paper on the state of this alpha species. This would be used by others to manage the fisheries. Natalie Scott had developed a highly sophisticated model to get a snapshot of the population at any point in time or space. She could not afford to be wrong.

The story starts just four months to either graduate in the time allotted, or not. In just weeks she would defend her preliminary findings in front of the most esteemed experts in her field of study. Nobody knew more about her subject matter than she did. Then there is a snag.

The story begins on the night February 13th, 2017, just as Natalie's population numbers are taking a sudden nose dive and suddenly her tagged tunas have gone off the radar. Her graphs depicting a gradual decline had dropped off as steeply as the cliff upon which the lab stood. She needed to find an explanation. Fast.

Natalie's love for science and the man in her life are hanging in the balance as she gets caught in a ruthless network of thugs on the high seas, far from where the eye can see.

Look for more adventures of Natalie Scott in the next sequel to "Hook, Line and Sinker."

Contact: info@earthadvertising.com

CHAPTER ONE
Ocean Center, La Jolla, California
February 14, 1 am

The campus was dark on Saturday night but for the ghostly hue of one computer screen that shone from the marine biology lab, perched high on the cliffs over Black's Beach. The day's chorus of clanging scuba gear, beeping machinery, sloshing wave tanks and grinding core samples had long given way to the evening's soft snore of aquarium pumps and waves dissipating calmly on La Jolla's sandy shore.

Marine biology student Natalie Scott sat alone in the lab, scrolling through her data in exhaustion. She was searching for a clue, or a miracle, to help decipher what the numbers were trying to tell her about the world's Pacific bluefin tuna populations. So far, she lacked a reasonable scientific explanation for the sudden disappearance of this remarkable super species, the subject matter of her PhD thesis. They'd gone off her radar in a matter of weeks. Not months, not years, not decades. Weeks.

It had been almost eight years that she'd been studying bluefin as her topic at the Ocean Center. Natalie's bluefin population models had predicted a sloping rate of decline but this was ridiculous. It was just her kind of luck to have the numbers go haywire just months before she needed the thesis to be signed off by her advisory board. One of the ocean's largest pelagic fish were gone missing and nobody was going to believe her. It was probably a glitch in the data. Something she had overlooked. How could a species that had roamed the sea for millions of years longer than man suddenly be gone? She knew the breeding and feeding patterns of these magnificent creatures like the back of her hand. There should be 40,000 adults left at the very least.

Her dream of being a marine biologist was becoming a nightmare. Hadn't it already cost Natalie her marriage? For one thing, she was almost 29 years old and still living on Top Ramen. Her fisheries grant had run dry. The U.S. government had cut all funding to the Food Chain Group, where her lab was housed. But they seemed to have plenty of money to spend on fishing subsidies, to say nothing of oil and mineral exploration. The Geology Department was living high on the hog. Huh, she thought. My epitaph will read: I tried to save the world but it killed me. While Americans going to war over oil were well funded, those waging war against extinction struggled to put food on the plate.

Natalie Scott wanted to get on with her life. What stood between her and the wide world outside the oceanographic institution were the five signatures of her advisory board that she needed for the institution to accept her PhD thesis. Her five thesis advisors were among the most respected oceanographers in the field and none of them signed off on a thesis nonchalantly. It was their scientific reputation on the line as much as hers. This is the price you pay for being at the top of your game. Getting accepted was competitive. Getting out was an even greater hurdle. There was a time limit, too, and she was approaching it fast. Betty in Graduate Administration had sent her a notice to say that unless she finished this semester, she'd need to repeat some graduate courses again due to a statute of limitations. Refresher courses, they called them. Her coursework credits would begin to expire. Like the natural world, academia was survival of the fittest. She was beginning to question whether she was among the fit. She was stuck in a rut and she knew it.

As the moon came up over the pier, it illuminated the bright yellow sun on the *Endless Summer* poster pinned to her bulletin board. The moon's pale light spilled onto computer printouts, piles of graphs, open books, maps, and diagrams all over the lab. Taped to the walls were illustrated posters of every migratory species of large saltwater fish known to man. Caught by the moonlight, the white chalk on her blackboard took on an eerie glow. Coffee mugs and food wrappers were strewn around the place and reams of paper overflowed from the recycle bin.

Natalie broke her gaze on the computer screen and stared out to sea, its frenetic surface reflecting the moon back up to the sky, accentuating the boundary between air and sea, between what can be seen and what remains to be seen.

Her mind descended down an old familiar rabbit hole. No wonder Chad had left her. Look at her now, surrounded by fish data. No, *drowning* in fish data. Large pelagic migratory fish data. Her thoughts took the spiraling route they had traveled over and over again so many times in the past six months. Back to the night she missed the opening of the Underwater Film Club's exhibit at La Jolla Museum of Art while waiting in the lab for signals from her tagged tuna. That fateful night when her husband, the love of her life, met 'the other girl.' She wasn't just any girl either. To drive a spear through Natalie's heart, she was a beautiful, talented underwater photographer with plenty of time on her hands and not a care in the world. "She's in the Underwater Hall of Fame," her husband boasted, as if that made it ok. Funny, how life can bite you in the butt. The rumor was that he told her they were separated. Huh! Odd, he hadn't mentioned anything that very morning when she surprised him with breakfast in bed. Blueberry pancakes.

Natalie had met Chad on a tagging trip offshore of the Baja where bluefin liked to congregate. He was the boat mechanic. The crew watched as he circled her, closer and closer, throughout the research expedition like something on Wild Kingdom. By the time the ship got back to port, he was making plans to visit her in La Jolla. They fell in love designing underwater housings together for the webcams she was hanging from her buoys to monitor the feeding grounds where bluefin liked to congregate known as the McDonalds of the deep. "And now, L-I-I-I-VE from the buoy, the secret life of bluefin tuna," Chad had announced as they first brought up the images on their Macs and posted them on You Tube. Within months they were married.

She was the one who got him his job as a marine tech at the Center. He soon became the sexy campus handyman who could fix just about anything. Anything, but their marriage. "He used to be mounting cameras, now he's mounting a photographer," Natalie would ruminate. If her brother Finn were alive, she imagined him punching Chad's lights out to defend her honor, or at least offering a shoulder to cry on. She felt completely alone.

17

A ring tone pierced the dark night and one of the square plastic buttons on the lab phone lit up yellow on her extension. Natalie pressed it and lifted the receiver. "Last call!!" screamed Debby through a noisy crowd. "Natalie, come out and party. It's Saturday night! Get your butt down here to the Gaslamp District. I would have called earlier but I lost my cell phone." Her roommate Debby, who had moved into the apartment she shared with Chad in Ocean Beach the day he moved out, was obviously drunk. Two sheets to the wind, in nautical terms.

Debby was tucked into a phone booth in downtown San Diego's tony Gaslamp District in a teeny tiny black dress and heels. Her Chinese looks were a guy magnet. Two preppies walked toward her, swaying a bit, and giving her the *needy* look that she was such a sucker for. Another full fraternity of them walked by and eyed her up and down hungrily, before turning the corner. She yelped into the phone all but bursting Natalie's eardrum.

Natalie put the call on speakerphone to protect her ears and free her hands. The yellow glow from the phone button cast a warm light on the silky cheeks of her beautiful face that was cast in pale blue by the computer screen upon which she became fixated again.

"Sorry, I can't," she told her best friend. "Dr. Jenkins is stopping by at noon to look over my calculations. If I can just get my freaking thesis done…"

Debby obviously was not listening, having lost her ability to focus. Natalie could hear the deep voices of guys in the background on the other end and her roommate's affected giggle and it was irritating. She raised her voice and her cheeks flushed with impatience. "If I can stick this out for four more months, I can get a life!"

Debby began singing *somewhere over the rain-bow* off key. "Seriously, Nat. There's some hot tuna down here. Come on! The fish are biting. It will get your mind off things. Have a little fun!"

Ever since Debby did her runaway bride thing a year ago, she'd been a little boy crazy. A lot boy crazy, actually. Natalie figured it was either because she had never dated anyone but Lian, or because after reversing her direction half way down the aisle in front of everybody she had some regrets. Lian, who would no longer answer her phone calls, was a nice smart guy from MIT with a promising future and she loved the guy and so did her parents. However, it was no time for Natalie to nurture Debby's complex inner feelings of abandonment that she instigated herself. She pushed him away Until Natalie finished her thesis, nothing could matter.

"I *can't* have fun. There's nothing fun about trying to pull two billion large pelagic fish out of a hat in a matter of weeks!" she yelled into the lab's speakerphone to her friend downtown, in a voice so loud she scared herself and raised her heart rate.

Debby was slurring by now. "Ok, seriously, girl, what are you talking about?"

"I said... if my calculations aren't right, they won't support my conclusions, and if my conclusions aren't supported, no PhD after all this. I'll be doing the dead man's float professionally.

I'm talking scrubbing tanks at Sea World for the rest of my life. I'll be mopping up penguin feces." Natalie wondered why she was even trying to explain herself to Debby who was obviously not feeling any sympathy, or anything at all for that matter. It was like talking to a fish.

Laughter and screaming relayed through the phone from downtown. "I just met this guy, Nat, and he stole my cellphone and won't give it back unless I have a drink with him. C'mon, Nat. You could be here in 20 minutes. And you could drive me home…"

A guy named Roy in a blue and white striped jersey and khakis knocked on the window of the phone booth, holding up Debby's cell phone in one hand and pointing to it with the other. He was mouthing the words, "Is this yours?"

"Give me that!" Debby screamed dropping the receiver, which swung like a snake by the tail, banging its head hard against the metal booth. Natalie was glad she was on speaker, or that would have really hurt. Debby fumbled with the receiver and returned her attention to Natalie.

"Nat, all I heard was something about thesis and feces and fishes and Sea World… are you ok?"

"Never mind. Have fun Debby, and save one for me. I'm hanging up now."

"Really?" Debby thought it wouldn't be too hard to bring a few guys home. There must have been a dozen guys per girl out tonight, and the odds were getting better as the night wore on.

"No, not *really*! It's bad enough that I wasted almost six years of my life married to Prince Charming. If I flunk my dissertation that's also six years of graduate school down the drain. I'm fish feed until I can explain how billions of large pelagic fish could be missing from the world's oceans without a scientific explanation."

"Nat, there are plenty of fish in the sea. Holy mackerel!" The guy named Roy in the blue-striped shirt held Debby's cell phone high in the air and headed into a bar. She dropped the phone again and chased him. The operator came on, "Please deposit... twenty… five… cents… Please… deposit… twenty…"

Natalie hung up and turned her attention back to the sea. Her nerves felt like a top spinning out of control. She hoped like heck that the flutter in her stomach, the pound in her heart, the ache in her throat, and the confusion in her brain were only temporary. That the fear of failure would subside so she could think clearly. Could it get worse? Is this the bottom? She struggled to count her blessings listing them one by one in her head.

She pictured a milk carton: MISSING: Pacific Bluefin Tuna. Last seen: February 14. Place: The Ocean. Characteristics: Swim in schools, follows the currents, breeds during so and so, and feeds on this and that. May travel with dolphins.

The moon had passed over the foothills and now the only light in the lab was her screen saver. Cartoon fish eating other fish, on down the food chain. She watched the seagulls land on the railing of the pier, then fly off into the night. Lulled by the waves and released by the freedom of gulls taking wing, she fell asleep.

CHAPTER TWO
Small apartment in Ocean Beach, San Diego
February 14, 2 a.m.

Debby staggered into the small Ocean Beach apartment that she now shared with Natalie. She was with Roy, the guy from the bar in the blue and white striped jersey. He nosed around the place as she opened the refrigerator and took out two beers. Roy inspected the photos hanging in a row down the hallway toward Natalie's room. He perused shots of a hot chick with colleagues on an oceanographic research vessel, posing with parents at graduation from Stanford, riding tandem on a windsurfer with what looked like her sister, and hanging upside down from a tree like possums with what looked a brother. Roy stopped at the last photo by the door of a happy Natalie in a teeny-weeny bikini posing with a surfboard at La Jolla Shores. Beyond the photos, a bedroom door was open and the bed was empty.

"Where's your roommate?" asked Roy.

"Natalie? She's a grad student up at The Ocean Center. She's getting down to the wire on her PhD. They told her if she didn't finish her thesis and get it signed by the end of April, it's back to the drawing board… do not pass go, do not collect PhD. So, that's pretty much all she does." Debby cocked her head in a cute pout. "Why, do you like her?"

"Is this a trick question?" he said with a twinkle in his eye as he surveyed Debby up and down.

"Well, I could fix you up. As of six months ago, she's available," Debby teased.

Roy gave a long hard look at Natalie's medium-sized breasts in the photo on the wall, and then turned to Debby's, which were pushing up and out of her little black dress giving them the illusion of huge. Or the vodka martinis were kicking in. "All I want to know is if you are. Are *you* available?"

"What's that supposed to mean?" Debby said tugging on his shirt to pull him closer.

"You gonna let me in?" he pleaded, gently positioning her face for a kiss with his fingertips.

"On the first date? I don't do one night stands," Debby said, holding his gaze up close and personal with her jet black eyes.

Roy's voice had become softer and more melodic. "I met you before midnight at the bar. We came to your apartment after midnight, which is technically the next day. That's the second date. Furthermore, you don't have to stand. You could lie down." Roy hugged her tight enough to tumble the two of them to the couch as one unit. They started making out and he ran his hands up her dress, only to encounter panty hose. "Who wears panty hose in San Diego?" he said.

"Me, because of guys like you," she returned. She drove a fingernail into his arm just hard enough to make it hurt but not bleed. "Oh, no you don't sailor. Like I said, not on the first date."

"Ok, what are you doing tonight?" he whispered, sucking on her earlobe.

"I told Natalie I'd go to her Friends of the River potluck tonight."

"Friends of the River, as opposed to enemies of the river?" He had begun to float his words lightly on his exhale into her ear and it made her tingle.

"It's a white water kayaking and rafting club," she said clasping his hands together to keep them out of her dress.

"Well, it sounds fishy, this white water rafting club. Maybe I'll just have to check it out, too."

"Sorry, that would break every law of girl's night out."

"So, arrest me. You got any handcuffs?"

Debby raised one eyebrow and looked him straight into the pupils. He got excited. Heck, maybe she was the kinky type after all. "No handcuffs, sorry. But I've got mace!" She hissed the last "s" syllable into his lips, removed his two hands from her top, one at a time, and gave each a playful slap.

CHAPTER THREE
Ginza District, Tokyo
February 14, 6 pm

It was the end of the business day for Tokyo's corporate workforce, nicknamed "salary men" for the repetition of their daily lives. They poured out of the trains and into the streets of the Ginza District, forming lines in front of its tony restaurants. A skyline of animated advertisements and film trailers towered above, creating a chaotic circus of reflections, projecting back and forth onto skyscrapers and bouncing off shop windows and the shiny sedans that crawled along Tokyo's most expensive neighborhood. Brightly lit department stores showcased designer purses encrusted with rare gems, exotic furs with the limbs intact, belt buckles of elephant tusks, and plastic creations with sticker-shock prices. All down the strip, Jaguars, Rolls Royces, Corvettes, and Ferraris were double and triple-parked.

With much fanfare, a bowing and nodding concierge opened the car door of a Mercedes limousine that had pulled up under the awning of the restaurant Uogashi. A distinguished elderly gentleman sporting a bright red cravat with matching handkerchief emerged from its belly and was ushered to the protection of the awning in front and into the foyer. On cue, a brigade of men in fine black suits stepped out of the town cars and shuffled in behind him. They moved in formation as one unit shuffling behind the elderly VIP. Inside Uogashi, crowds of executives from the auto, computer, manufacturing, aviation, shipping, pharma and other industries milled around the bar toasting one another's accomplishments of the day with shochus and kamikaze cocktails as they waited for tables. Sexy geisha girls in short silk brocade wraps and tight black boots circulated among them delivering cocktails.

The VIP and his brigade of men were escorted through Uogashi's entryway and down a private hallway to a host station where a maître d' greeted them. They were led to a sliding door of rice paper and bamboo. The party filed into a room lined with plush red sofas surrounding a low-lying bamboo table set lavishly for fifteen guests. The far wall was made of glass, behind which fish were swimming among artificial fluorescent marine vegetation. Maine lobsters and Alaskan king crabs crawled along the sandy bottom.

Reverence toward the VIP was obvious by the way the party of dinner guests hung their heads down in an exaggerated deep bow as he sat down. Delicate geisha girls with faces painted as porcelain dolls flowed into the room with decorative drinks and exotic appetizers, which were quickly circulated around the table. When the refreshments arrived, the expressions of the guests switched from reverent to jovial, all at once. As they consumed the food and drink, the geishas removed the plates and replaced them with dishes piled high with creatures, many of which looked to be still alive. The men devoured everything, eyes and all.

The distinguished older gentleman kept a stone face. He signaled the most delicate of the geisha girls, speculating on the happy ending this dinner might conclude with. Though speculative, it was quite possible that she might accompany him to the adjacent spa area for the shark fin soup. The seven delights of this house specialty, it was said, included the unwrapping of her kimono with great ceremony, and a series of provocations during which he would submit to the virile powers of the soup like a helpless boy under the influence. Now, he said something to her in a quiet undertone, which sent her scurrying off toward the kitchen.

Several miles away down by the docks where the fish auctions roared by day like Wall Street, all was quiet. In the shade of an enormous warehouse, an ice cream truck sat hidden from the security floodlights. The driver was playing Sudoku on his *keitai denwa,* cell phone, when its ring cut through the night like a cleaver. He nodded his head up and down at the phone, and then dialed another number. A massive door rolled up and he was summoned up the ramp and soon was driving into the vast guts of the building where an ocean of live, writhing fish was piled high. At the far end was a tank for prize fish with hefty seven-figure price tags.

Within minutes, the truck was winding through the back streets of Tokyo behind a black SUV

Nissan Pathfinder in which two security guards were sucking down cigarettes and casting them out the window, leaving a trail of red embers in their wake. The truck driver concentrated on the digital clock as the man who was riding shotgun nervously checked his watch. When they got to the Ginza District, they hit gridlock. An endless procession of bicycles, luxury automobiles, delivery trucks, wagons, yellow cabs and black sedans stretched before them. As far as they could see were green traffic lights that signaled "go" even though they could not. They were stuck. This pissed off the driver of the refrigerator truck to no end. He began to lean on the horn in an abusive "EEEE, EEEEE!" swearing in Japanese, "Fuhkkk." Losing his temper, he swung his truck around angrily with a screech. The sudden motion nearly tipped over the truck as the contents swashed to the outside of the turn. The Nissan Pathfinder followed. Through a nauseous trip of twists and turns accentuated by the effect of the swashing in the back, the two vehicles wove their way toward downtown Ginza using back alleys. They pulled another final sharp turn down an alley that ran behind the main drag. This nearly toppled the truck over, but it regained equilibrium and sped down the back alley for six more blocks.

Several armed security men stood in the dark lot behind the Uogashi's kitchen under a bare light bulb, waiting for the ice cream truck. Upon its arrival they drew their weapons to protect the delivery. The driver tucked a gun into his pocket and his passenger packed a pistol into his belt. He backed the truck up to the kitchen's back door where a crowd of workers had gathered with pitchforks. He set the brake, got out, and unlocked the lever on the refrigerated vault. Then he stood back and motioned the kitchen team to also step back. As he opened the hatch, a huge wave of icy seawater gushed out through the door into the asphalt. All of the men wrestled the contents contained in a huge net. An enormous live bluefin tuna was thrashing about, eyes wide with fear, the whites flashing in the darkness. It took seven men to maneuver the fish through the back door of the kitchen, its 15-foot length dwarfing them in size. There was an exchange of cash in black suitcases between the chef and the men in the black SUV. One and a half million dollars, paid in yen, to be precise.

CHAPTER FOUR
Marine Biology Lab
February 14, 2 am

Back in the lab, Natalie had dozed off. Theories to support her research findings were swimming around and around in her brain like a goldfish banging its head against its bowl.

She woke up in a sweat to the blinking light on the lab phone followed by a ring that stung her senses like the clang of the buoy bell right in between her ears. It was probably Debby calling again. She decided to ignore it.

This wasn't the life she had imagined when she first received her letter of acceptance from what she still thought was the most prestigious oceanographic institution in the world. She had imagined herself as a sexy and tan marine biologist with sun-bleached hair in a teeny-weeny bikini on a tropical island. When she met Chad, he became part of the dream. Then, it was the two of them dreaming together as they lay entangled at night, the stars their candlelight, and the waft of gardenias and honeysuckle their perfume.

Ever since she was a little girl Natalie had wanted to study the sea. Her childhood's most cherished moments were the sunrise walks along the beaches of Martha's Vineyard at her grandparent's house with her father. Sometimes she slept in her jumper so she could launch out of bed at the slightest hint of dawn or the creak in the old house signaling that her dad was going to walk their dog. These early strolls together on the beach were reverently quiet and magical. Together they would study the surf breaking on the sand and hypothesize where the waves had originated based upon their angle to the beach, the speed and distance between crests, and the ripple patterns in the sand. "The Azores," he might say. Or, "Newfoundland." Or, "Bermuda." She loved the way he squinted his eyes and stared in the direction of the sea whenever he was thinking.

The damn phone rang again. She picked it up and yelled into the little pinholes. "Leave me the freakin' alone, Deb! You're wasted. I'm not partying tonight ok? Get that into your cute little Chinese head!"

A deep and familiar voice answered back. "Natty?"

"Dad?" How weird. She had just been thinking about him. What time was it back East? "Dad, what time is it back there? Is everything alright?"

"That's what I was going to ask you. I tried you at home and nobody answered. I was already up, so I thought I'd try the lab. And there you are! My princess of the sea."

Her throat ached at the sound of his words, and it made her vocal chords cramp. "Boy, dad, is it nice to hear your voice." Natalie thought about how her parents kept one clock set to West Coast time zone, PST, to remember her by.

"Well, your mom's asleep and I got up to check the furnace. It's freezing here." He paused, drawing her in. "Natty? Is my little baby girl ok? Natty?"

The longer she struggled to reply, the more her throat cramped and the more awkward the silence. Her eyes began to burn and then give way to tears. An ache ran from her temples to her guts. The lump in her throat made her glands swell, and her ears tweak. Pressure built in her solar plexus as she fought all her emotions back down to the depths of her being where they had been lurking ever since her divorce. The cavern of darkness that echoed, "you chose him, I told you so," in a mean Gollum-from-the-Hobbit voice reminding her that she was not good enough for a love story with a happy ending. She thought about her grandmother and her mother who had taught her to always see the bright side. "And always act like a lady," her aunt would always pipe in. Where were the ladies in the family when she needed them? Most had passed away and her mom was now living in a world of her own where she hardly recognized her. Both her mom and her dad were venturing into the world of dementia together, but her mom was further along. At times Natalie became a distant memory and not a real person.

Her dad’s voice on the phone brought back happy memories of childhood, when she had not a care in the world. It teased her back to the age of innocence. A parade of memories marched through her mind. Thumbing through the lawn with her brother Finn to find four-leaf clovers. Knitting winter scarves with her Nana. Ironing fresh linens with her mom. The first crocus of spring poking through the snow below the kitchen window. The happy sound of applause when they announced her name at the State Spelling Bee Championship, and the pitter-patter of her heart when Billy Rogers snuck a valentine in her lunchbox. It was a yard sale of stuff as though caught in the path of a tornado, and then whipped around like Dorothy's house in the Wizard of Oz.

She snapped out of it, like flipping off a television set. Her dad was still talking. He was asking about Chad again. He would not allow himself to comprehend that his daughter was really divorced. Natalie didn’t have the heart to keep correcting him after a while. He was protecting his heart is all, and maybe thought he was protecting her too. She loved him for it. He was simply creating a new world for himself where down was up, back was forward, and everything was ok. In this new world, Natalie was married to Chad, a boat captain at The Center for Oceanography.

Funny, Chad was to blame for the 'boat captain' story, which was a lie. Her dad had bought his pumped up job description - hook, line and sinker. It was a yarn that Natalie had allowed her husband to spin, in the interest of his ego. One he had spun to elevate himself from his real profession as a marine handy man who fixed broken equipment around campus. She had no reason to challenge her dad's fictional image of who Chad was. His mind was free to travel wherever it wanted to, in a land of no space or time. It was his right. She wanted most of all for her dad to be happy. Her sister Sally had a different opinion on how to handle the memory loss of their mom and dad. Sally insisted on getting them back on track by helping get the facts straight. Natalie didn't see the point. Her dad had begun to take his imagination to whole new levels and it kept him sane in a weird way. She didn't encourage it, but she allowed it.

Mr. Scott waited patiently on the other end of the line. Natalie struggled to flip off her mental television again to focus on the conversation. "Well, dad, it's just this thesis."

She could barely suppress her gulp for air and a sniffle that was building up in her sinuses. Breathe, she thought. Breathe. She already wished she could hit rewind in this conversation and take back the reference to her thesis. There was no reason to tell him about the problems in her research. He'd want to help her but he couldn't. Nobody could. Not even her review committee. Why should she make them all miserable? In her family, the women were the happy makers and had been for hundreds if not thousands of years.

Her dad's voice snapped her back to the phone again. "Nattie? Tell me about your thesis."

"There are problems with my thesis, dad. And the graduate administration office says I'm running out of time. If I don't get it done by April, it's back to the drawing board, including refresher classes. More school, and no income. I'm sorry dad. I'm sorry I brought it up. Everything's fine. Really great, actually. How are you?"

"Let's put our heads together," he said in a voice that felt like God. "Together we can conquer the world! What exactly is holding up your thesis?"

"A plausible explanation for why my bluefin tuna data is deviating from my predictions. It's not the gentle slope I predicted, dad. It's a cliff. I've combed through thousands of data entry points, over and over again and it's like someone pulled the plug and they got sucked down a drain."

"What is your hypothesis?" He suddenly sounded like good ole' dad. Receptive, alert, intelligent, and pondering. She wished she could see him pondering right now. His listening stance and signature squint were as comforting as chicken soup.

Hypothesis? She didn't have a good one. An explanation she could validate. Natalie took a huge big breath of air, filling her lungs with fresh *prana*, as her yoga teacher called it. "Well, there's always climate change! The escalated rate of burning gas and trees and trash and everything else since the industrial revolution has caused the planet's climate to spin out of whack very quickly. Ice at the poles are thinning in most places and land glaciers are losing their integrity as rivers form and gush underneath them. In Greenland and Antarctica for instance, when these icy cold streams reach the sea, they sink as dense currents that flow along the seafloor, displacing the warmer waters. Meanwhile the Northwest Passage is opening up, and the Northeast Passage, too. The circulation patterns are changing very quickly. Maybe they are hiding somewhere."

Natalie realized how ridiculous that sounded and was glad she was practicing her on her dad and not her advisors. But, she pressed on.

"My colleagues over in Physical Oceanography say it's like a washing machine up in the Arctic right now like nothing we've ever seen in the historical records. The geologic record, yes. But, man's history record, no.

'See, dad, I know these new patterns are forcing changes in the migration patterns of pelagic fish. Feeding and spawning locations are moving around. But honestly, climate change is not enough to take them off the radar completely! I'm beginning to suspect that I'm not getting accurate data from the industrial fishing industry. My numbers aren't adding up. The dilemma is that my advisors are depending on me to be the expert, the one who has it all figured out. But, I don't. That's the problem, dad. I don't have it all figured out. I did, but now I don't."

He gave her his familiar, *uh huh,* so she went on.

'It's plausible that tuna may be traveling in the resulting new currents like a roller coaster. Or, hey, maybe they are all hiding in a deep submarine trench somewhere. I would! How am I supposed to know? All I know is that they've fallen off my radar and I'm the one who has been monitoring this species for the past six years. Hey, maybe they're smart enough to hide from the industrial fishing industry's gazillion dollar, *subsidized* tracking technology, which is funded by rogue governments. The United Nations is trying but has not yet succeeded in protecting the high seas from piracy, so the area of the deep sea beyond national jurisdiction is a free for all. Fish up for grabs. Winner takes all. In short, I've lost the signal on my tagged tuna, dad."

Natalie had worked herself up into a frenzy. She was driving herself right off the deep end. But she knew she was right. That's what was driving her nuts. The climate had been fairly stable for 10,000 years and now the changes on Earth were happening so rapidly that it makes sense for the animal kingdom to have to adjust. With climate change, harmful chemicals, plastic pollution, acidification, overfishing and a host of other manmade plagues, the sea was at risk of collapse. Large pelagic migratory species were disappearing exponentially leaving the bottom of the food chain free to flourish out of control. But the bluefin were disappearing even faster than predicted. This abrupt disappearance had thrown her for a loop. So this is what it feels like to go bonkers, she thought.

Her dad's voice awoke her from the dialogue that plagues even the most diligent of scientists. "Well, are you asking my opinion?" he asked, snapping her to the present and the problem at hand. "I just want to support you. I'm here as your ballast and #1 fan."

"Of course your opinion is valued, dad. But no offense, it's probably something I've already thought of," she said cautiously fearing this could be misunderstood.

"Then just act surprised!" he laughed. "An old guy like me needs to feel like a smarty pants sometimes."

They both laughed, enjoying being mentally connected and together again, even if just on the phone. "Ok, shoot," she said beginning to feel better.

"Nat, your research isn't about global warming and you'd still be getting a read on the tags, wouldn't you? How deep can you get a signal? Leave climate change to the atmospheric crowd. There are plenty of people focusing on that. You got NOAA, NASA, the IPCC, and every meteorologist under the sun measuring that stuff. You simply have to present your data on the population of large pelagic fish. Stick to the bluefin. You've got to isolate these things. You've taken the whole world on your shoulders, honey. Just the bluefin, ok? And skip the sharks. Forget about them. They are a whole other story. They're getting slaughtered finned and drowned in droves. These are gangsters. That's dangerous stuff to interfere with, cupcake."

Mr. Scott was roaming around his house as he spoke, wearing the headphone set that Natalie had given him for Christmas. He was a hobby scientist who often knew more about the world than academics. He read a lot. His naturally curious mind was a trait he had inherited from his own dad, and passed on the Natalie. She'd also inherited his wife's good looks. As he spoke, he looked at the photos hanging on the polished wooden walls. Pictures of Natalie, his eldest daughter Sally and deceased son Finn. The photos of him, which had gnawed at him like a tiger for so many years, were now a comforting reminder of the times they had spent together. Finn had been a wild child and Mr. Scott was now, ten years after his death, finally at peace with his destiny. Above the photos was a shelf of trophies draped with ribbons in blue, red, yellow and white from swim meets and other tournaments. He and his wife had retired and moved into his childhood summerhouse. It was a two-story ranch house just across a dirt road from the Nantucket Sound. The road was the main artery to the other homes up the beach, and it was eroding. Mr. Scott had become a global warming closet scientist, obsessively reading literature predicting the rate of sea level change along New England's broad continental shelf that was strewn with the glacial moraine that had formed Cape Cod and the Islands.

"Just get out there and find those fish!" he said, staring out the big picture window to the sea.

Duh, she thought. And in less than three months. "I just feel lost, dad. With Chad gone and all, too," she said forgetting that he didn't accept the truth that she wasn't married anymore. "This always was supposed to be something we were doing together."

"Just make Chad some of that nice hot soup your mother makes," he said. "What's it called?"

"Goulash?"

"Yes, just make Chad some goulash. Then go find those fish!"

"Thanks dad. You get some sleep, ok? And give mom a kiss from me."

"Good night my little mermaid."

As Natalie spoke *I love you* into the phone, she heard his end hang up. At least he had finally mastered the new headset.

Natalie put her head down, tears spilling onto the charts and graphs all over her desk, leaving pools of blue ink. She fell asleep.

The reflection of her screen saver of fish eating fish eating fish eating fish played on her face as she slept and reflected off the lab window. Visions of large pelagic fish thrashed in her head. The buoy bell off La Jolla Shores clanged as the swell picked up a bit. Like a phonograph needle guided by the grooves in a vinyl record, the thoughts in her slumber followed the data graphs that were now engraved in her mind. Tens of thousands of fish that she couldn't account for, and less than three months left to figure it out.

As if in *seek* mode, her thoughts skipped over every injustice she'd ever experienced that had collected in her brain over time and were being stored in some dark matter. It was as if she was programmed unconsciously to seek doom and gloom lately. There was Mr. Broody from junior high who told her that she'd never be more than a housewife so she'd better be good at it. That girls were born to breed and she'd better not screw it up. When she couldn't name the parts of a flower involved in pollination, Mr. Broody humiliated her. "The stamen," he yelled in her direction, "is the flower's penis, Ms. Scott. Would someone like to tell Natalie about the birds and the bees?" To this day her face burned red and prickly just remembering. She was vulnerable to self-identifying as the kid at the bottom of the food chain.

Her brother Finn had used this as fodder to tease her, hiding dead bees in her food to reopen the wound. Right up until the day of his accident. The loss of Finn dragged at her heart despite all the grievance group sessions. He was instantly deleted from her life by a stupid boating accident. Her mom and dad were left to spend the rest of their lives imagining what he might have become.

She understood forgiveness. It was becoming her mantra and was now even trickling into her thoughts about Chad. She got the message. The most powerful thing to do is forgive.

When she allowed herself to feel the terrible loss of her brother, she missed him badly. She wondered if they would grow to become best friends. Allies in a world that can be heartless.

The sensation of free falling took over her dreams. She was grabbing for branches to break her fall. But in reality, Natalie was infinitely stronger than she gave herself credit for.

CHAPTER FIVE
February 14, 7 am
Ocean Beach, San Diego

The sun made its way through a slit between the curtains in Debby's room and pecked at her lids and this woke her up. She squinted to summon scenes from the night before. Once she realized where she was, she was relieved to be in her own bed but still didn't remember getting there. She tiptoed quietly to the bathroom for aspirin and water, stopping to poke her head into Natalie's room. It was empty. She called the lab.

Back in the lab, Natalie was still at her desk crunching numbers again. She saw the button light up her extension on the old telephone that didn't offer the benefit of caller ID. "Dad? You shouldn't worry about me. I was distraught last night when you called. Just overtired. Everything's great. But I miss you."

"It's me, Debby. Your room mate? Nat. I'm the one worried about you."

"I'm okay I guess. It's not just the thesis. I wasn't supposed to be alone during this. It was Chad's idea to finish my degree, and then he ran off with that…"

Debby rolled her eyes at the phone, causing pain in the brain. She'd nearly run out of patience talking about Chad. Holding the receiver to her hurting head, she scanned the apartment looking for any signs that would jog her memory and reconcile a history of the night before. "Don't go there, girlfriend. C'mon, get over him, Nat. He's a loser with a capital L…" She held a big L with thumb and forefinger to her forehead.

From the living room came a voice. Roy, who had slept on the sofa in his clothes, was heard stumbling around looking for his shoes. "Who, me?"

Debby had forgotten about him. "I gotta get going," he called, feeling awkward. "Thanks for the accommodations. I'll call you." With that, she heard the door shut. Ouch, again.

Debby turned to her phone and got serious. "Let me ask you something, Natalie. Do you really wish you were that slutty photographer he ran off with? You think he's gonna stay with her? And what about her? He lied to her about being married. Eventually she'll see that."

Natalie winced just thinking of them together. It was still a fresh wound. "But what if he does? I don't think I could bear it." Her eyes filled with tears again and that haunting ache in her gut came back.

As usual, Debby was hardheaded about this even though at the moment her head hurt. "Believe me, you can bear it. You seem to forget how uncomfortable it was taking him to parties. Remember that time he tried to pick up your lab partner? Besides YOU dumped HIM! He didn't dump you."

Natalie protested. "But he started it…"

"And you ended it, with good reason. It was one of the smartest things you've ever done, Miss-full-scholarship-to-Stanford. It's history and you have to move on. Don't start thinking it was going to get better."

"But if it weren't for my focus on the PhD, we'd be in the tropics together living the life. I'd give anything to be a cocktail waitress at some old thatched roof beach bar right now. Chad could fix outboards while I served Pina Coladas with a flower in my hair," she said, not able to let go of this vision of paradise.

Debby stopped her right there. "Stop! Tell me what you have to do, and by when? Just pull yourself together RIGHT NOW!" she said in a way that left no room for argument.

Natalie appreciated the take-no-prisoners attitude of her ballbuster friend. There was no truth whatsoever that china dolls were submissive pushovers. She'd never known any girl as tough as Deb, even though she weighed in at ninety-eight pounds. Natalie snapped out of her self pity as though struck by lightning.

"Ok, let's see. At noon today, my key advisor is coming to review my research and look over my best interpretation of the present state of bluefin population. The data curve happily zigzags for hundreds of years, takes a gentle but steady dive in the last twenty, and then just as my thesis is due, it free falls to zero. In fact, worse. My graph nosedives right down through the X axis. Hell, I'm getting negative numbers in my predictions, Deb. You can't have less than zero fish. There is an unexplainable plunge just as I was hoping to get the hell out of here. Nothing makes sense. My review committee surely won't accept this phenomenon without a scientific explanation. Yet, the catch figures from the fishing industry don't match up."

Her roommate was floundering. Debby thought hard, even though it really pinched her brain. "Ok, I've got three very powerful words for you. Two-week extension. In fact, is two-week one word? Great, make that two very powerful words. Tell the dude you need to do some more research. Isn't that what scientists always say?"

Natalie stood up to stretch, and consider this idea. "You know what, girlfriend, that's not a bad idea. But it will still only buy me, correction, *borrow me*, two weeks at the max and doesn't change my deadline. All five members of my committee have to give me a nod of approval before I waste my time on a final draft. His nod comes first."

"Two weeks is two weeks. Ask them to give you two weeks." This wasn't the first time Debby had to pull her friend off the ledge, in a manner of speaking. Deb had always been the "don't jump" voice of reason. That was her lot in life with a best friend who was a Type A genius, who lacked coping skills for disappointments. She snuggled back into her soft bed and settled her poor pounding head back onto her pillow.

As she considered Debby's advice to borrow more time, Natalie had a full-on panic attack. It made her heart race because she knew that an extension was no life raft. Her body was telling her to fight, flee or freeze, for which exercise was her only cure. A sprint down the beach would steady her mood and clear her head before she went about cancelling any meetings. It was still early. She could reach Dr. Jenkins when she got back, before he left his house. "I gotta go," said Natalie to Debby. "So you're coming with me to the Friends of the River to-night?"

Debby curled up in a fetal position within the womb of her down comforter, and cradled the phone. "Sure, I'm coming. Will there be any guys there?"

Natalie pondered this a moment, envisioning the membership of Friends of the River, a diverse cast of characters who shared only one thing in common– their love of whitewater. "Probably the same old, same old."

Debby groaned, "You're a real sparkplug, you know it? Let's just get margaritas at happy hour downtown."

Natalie furrowed her brow with a grave look of responsibility. "No, I'm on the spring white-water committee for the trip down the Kern River, planned for when they let out the dam sometime around Memorial Day. We at least have to stop by and check in. By the way we need to bring a dish. It's potluck." Little did she know that her roomie had to suppress a gag reflux at the mere mention of food, due to her fragile state with alcohol still reeling through her bloodstream.

"Ug" said Debby, "A potluck with river rats. It's ok this time but you better get out of your shell and live a little. You're young. You're beautiful. You dodged a bullet with that creep Chad and should celebrate that every minute of every day. By the way, Happy Valentine's Day."

Valentine's Day. The worst holiday of them all. It wasn't just Natalie's single status that made her despise Valentine's Day. It was the day that she first had a hint about her husband's affair. He'd been acting strange the day before and then a receipt from a florist fell out of his pocket when she was doing the laundry. The delivery address was in La Jolla on Nautilus Street. On Valentine's Day she waited to see what clever surprise he had up his sleeve for her that would take them to Nautilus Street. All day long, nothing happened. Not even a dinner invitation. In fact, he never came home.

As she hung up the phone with Debby, she muttered, “Ug, Valentine’s Day.”

Chapter SIX
Marine Biology Lab
February 14, 8 am

In the refreshing chill of early dawn, Natalie left the lab to take a run and clear her head. She did her stretches against the railing at the top of the stairs that lead down the cliff to the beach. The sun was peeking through Rattlesnake Canyon to the east and illuminating the bronze faces of surfers who were strung out just beyond the surf break straddling their boards and waiting for a set. Her shadow was elongated by the sun so low in the sky, Natalie hopped down the steep flight of steps, jogged across the service yard, down the boat ramp, past the dive locker, under the pier, and then she sprinted at top speed down the beach.

The surfers watched Natalie run length of La Jolla Shores toward the cove where the beach ended at the cliffs, and then turn around and run back. Back at the pier, she stretched her quads again against the piling. Then she sprinted back up the ramp, past the dive locker, across the service yard and up the steep stairway etched into the sandstone cliffs into which the Marine Biology Lab was imbedded. The stairway was made up of 200 steep steps, broken up by three landings. It ascended 150 feet making it a popular exercise circuit for joggers. Several of the surfers watched her with intrigue as Natalie ran up the first two flights and caught her breath on the second landing. She was a hottie who had been a familiar sight at the Shores for more than five years. From hot surfer chick in a bikini, to a swooning newlywed, to a melancholy married woman, to a distraught divorcee. They knew what happened and they all knew who the home wrecker chick was. Intimately. Chad was a jerk.

Back in the lab the coffee machine's light was on, signaling that even though it was Sunday morning, someone else was already at work and had come in while she was gone. Another wretched soul, she thought. The life of a grad student was pretty much 24/7 if you wanted to graduate in the time allotted. What time was it? The second hand of the old round clock that hung crooked on the wall marked time around its circumference. The minute hand worked its way to 12, as the hour hand landed on 9. This signaled that she only had three more hours until her advisor showed up. And she still had time to cancel.

Natalie flipped on the overhead fluorescent lights and rinsed out a coffee mug in the sink. The mug showcased a fishhook and read 'hooked on coffee.' With the mug in one hand and thick white chalk in the other, she stood before the blackboard and began to sketch complex systems of ocean currents circulating around the continents. She was looking for a clue as to what might have caused her subject matter to drop off the radar. It was 11 am when she was startled out of her wits by the sound of someone behind her, sending her third cup of coffee crashing to the floor.

“What you got here?” said an amused Dr. Jenkins, her key advisor. He was studying her drawings in great detail.

Her graduate advisor’s voice set off an alarm that reverberated throughout her central nervous system, which activated another bout of panic. Fight, flee… or freeze. If she were a fish, she would have changed color. She would camouflage into the surroundings of the lab. She'd disappear into the chalkboard, papers, posters, computer screen and coffee machine against the blue background of the sea.

Perhaps what separates humans is the fourth "f." Fight, flee, freeze or fudge-it. She had forgotten to cancel their meeting because she was too caught up in her head. Not only that, he was early. She wasn't prepared to defend her thesis. Not yet. Not by a long shot. Even the extra hour before their scheduled meeting at noon might have helped her to save face. "How long have you been here?" she quivered.

"About two and a half hours, on and off," he said. "I saw your car in the lot pretty early this morning. Were you here all night?"

"Uh, well, no, of course not. I mean yes. Yes, I was Dr. Jenkins. What are you doing here so early?"

His eyes looked at the floor as he referenced the laboratory's basement where many of the fish species thrived and spawned in perfectly tempered tanks. "I got an alert on my cell phone that one of the pumps was down, and came in to check it out. Don't want to lose any of our breeders, do we? Those spawners are the lifeblood of the lab. It turns out I had to jerry-rig a new fan belt. It used to be Chad's job, but he stopped answering his cell phone. Heard from him lately?"

At the mention of Chad's name, Natalie's face flushed and Dr. Jenkins realized he'd said something terribly, terribly wrong. He struggled to change the topic, looking to her chalk drawings. "Tell me about these drawings, Natalie." He smiled with a deep kindness that eased the situation. She was grateful that her advisor was a really good guy beneath his veneer of taskmaster. Some of the other grad students would be happy to send their own advisors to sea in a ship, and pour water in its gas tank. The sensitivity gene was often suppressed in scientists who by their very nature focused on facts and theory. She trusted him.

Jenkins studied the complex drawings as he spoke. “It looks like you’re planning an escape route from prison,” he said scratching his head, and running a hand through his silver hair. He looked perplexed.

Natalie’s face flushed even brighter red this time. It wasn't unusual for brainy people to put both feet in their mouth in one conversation, and Dr. Jenkins was no exception. It was never on purpose. He realized he’d done it again, though not sure exactly how.

Distraught, Natalie busied herself cleaning up the broken shards of the hooked-on-coffee mug while she gained her composure. So much for an extension. Here he was, an hour early and things were not going very well. Not very well at all. Ok, fight, flee, freeze or fudge-it. But first of all, focus.

“Dr. Jenkins,” she said, wringing coffee out of the sponge and cutting her hand on a shard without missing a beat. “I was just about to call you to cancel our meeting today. I need a little more time.” She thought back to her call with

Debby. “Two more weeks would allow me to fine-tune my preliminary thesis presentation to the advisory board.”

Dr. Douglas Jenkins was the head of the Center's marine biology department, in which the Food chain group was housed. During his tenure at the Center, he had graduated nearly two dozen grad students. This wasn’t the first time he’d seen a student freak out during their last semester and it wouldn’t be the last. A surprising number of them dropped out at this precise stage. It didn’t look good on the record to lose students after the institution had invested so much in these kids. The Center for Oceanography was very selective about who they let in, because they were trying to produce the best scientists in the world. Endurance was a factor. His peers in the global scientific community were counting on his department to go forth and multiply. He saw the next generation of scientists as his moral obligation. Yet, he could neither lower the standards for graduation, nor allow his prodigies to give up. In a sense they were in a symbiotic relationship.

"Well, you may be in luck," said Jenkins, studying the blackboard. "I'm inviting you to the International Tuna Convention in Paris, next week. We can postpone your presentation to the advisors until you return. Fisheries is footing the bill for you so I am hoping you'll come along and get informal feedback on your research from the fisheries community. I can move your first presentation to the advisory board to March 7, at 7 pm. Does that help? Consider it a field study. It's surprising how much data you can pick up at the side events during these conferences. Pillow talk at the bar. You'd be amazed what these industrial fishing fleet tycoons are willing to boast about after a few martinis."

Natalie kept waiting for a place to interrupt, but he kept going. Obviously he was set on her attendance. It might not even be negotiable. Just what she needed. To waste a week listening to people at the podium. One sage on stage after another. She raced to think of an excuse not to go as he kept talking.

"I'll order up a ticket for you. Fisheries will foot the bill and the conference might shed light on all this," he said, studying the chalkboard. "What is all this?"

Natalie seized the opportunity to interject. "Moving my presentation would be great, Dr. Jenkins. Thank you and March 7 sounds perfect." At the computer, she opened Google docs to move the date back three weeks on the advisory board's shared calendar. She moved the entry for *Natalie Scott, PhD candidate Thesis Progress Report "Trends in Pacific Bluefin Tuna Populations: Theories on Population Density and Migratory Patterns"* to Monday, March 7, 7 pm. She still hadn't settled on a name for her thesis.

Natalie began to explain to Dr. Jenkins why she shouldn't go to the conference. "Between now and then I need to focus on the research presentation. That will only give me seven more weeks to pass in a final draft after the feedback. Admin is threatening to expire my course credits if I don't graduate. This is my last hurrah, Dr. Jenkins. Fall semester just isn't an option for me. I'm living on fumes at this point. My roommate had to cover the utility bill this month."

Natalie had been to lots of these fisheries conferences over the years. It was populated by an alarming number of pompous men trying to pick up desperate grad students by offering them jobs in the fishing industry. "Dr. Jenkins. I've really got to figure this out."

She turned her attention to the blackboard where she had drawn the new current that had just spurted through the Northwest Passage, after having been frozen over for most of the last 10,000 years. Super-outfitted fishing fleets from US, Canada, Russia, Japan, Spain and China and other countries were already squeezing through there in summer. It was the new Panama Canal of the Arctic. She had no other explanation for a disruption in migration-as-usual for the majestic schools of bluefin, or where her tags were.

Breathe, she thought and then inhaled very deeply. She started by reviewing some statistics. Now she elaborated on her dilemma. "The abundance of spawning-size fish had declined over 60% since by 1970 to a barely sustainable level. It dropped off sharply until 1980 and then leveled off. I was still picking up signals from tagged fish until last month. Now there are none."

When I began my thesis, the Atlantic bluefin populations had reached a minimum level at which a moratorium was needed to stop them from going the way of the West African Black Rhino, the Tasmanian Tiger and other species now only found in museums. As you recall, the alarm was sounded. The Atlantic population declined to the brink of extinction, compounded by the oil spill in the Gulf of Mexico unfortunately just when the eggs and larva would be drifting into the Gulf to mature. At the last minute, an agreement was reached and the Atlantic bluefin started making a comeback. Fishing stopped just at the point of no return. Now, thirteen conservation groups had filed a petition to protect the Pacific bluefin tuna under the U.S. Endangered Species Act."

She kept going.

"Dr. Jenkins. I'm not getting a signal on the Pacifics anymore. Yet the fish markets are still reporting sales. Though my predictions anticipated a steep decline, these majestic intelligent creatures are now 'off the charts.' Below zero, Dr. Jenkins. But if you look at the sales data you'd think there was a more gradual, though plunging, decline. My research shows the population expectancy for the bluefin to be negative. My graph dipped below zero. So how can they be selling so many?

"I've tried to confirm the authenticity of the catch numbers, and match them to the market numbers, fresh, frozen, canned, dried, salted, and smoked... even cat food. The fecundity of each species is run against the fish lengths to predict the fertility rate of the bluefin, and what we can expect for juveniles, if the spawners are released. But, suddenly I can't get a read on the size of the population, even to the very best of my ability. The tagging project was picking up data. But ever since last month, I can't pick up anything. I was aware of the depletion of the fish stock, but what I'm trying to say is…" Her face flushed and she stopped dead in her tracks.

"Try me," he said, sounding surprisingly like her dad. "I won't bite."

"I have no idea where these schools are now, whether Atlantic or Pacific Bluefin. The Pacific bluefin aren't congregating around the buoys in the known feeding grounds, and they aren't picked up in the feeding grounds of the vast blue *Serengeti* of the Pacific you see here," she said sweeping her hand across the Northern Pacific. "Or the spawning grounds here," she said motioning to the Sea of Japan. "So, in desperation, I'm trying to explain their disappearance as the result of a radical shift in their feeding, breeding, spawning and migratory patterns that may have literally taken them off the radar beyond our instrumentation. Last year enough bluefin were caught, to fill a dozen Boeing 747s."

"Gulfstreams," he said with a knowing nod.

She continued, "You are right. The Gulfstream current is leaking into the Northwest Passage instead of turning around off the coast of Ireland which may affect the Atlantic bluefin, but what about Pacifics?"

Dr. Jenkins interrupted. "No, I meant Gulfstream *jets*. They use Gulfstream P-17s, not Boeings to cart the writhing, breathing tuna to posh restaurants. From ocean to table in under three hours. If these fish are delivered alive, they're worth $500/pound. That's not chump change. It'll buy you a lot of jets." He pointed to an old newspaper article on her poster board.. "They sold a half-ton bluefin in Tokyo for $1.76 million. Maybe your tagging project is simply leading the pirates of the sea to the treasure." He paused to let the thought sink in. "So will you come to the conference now?"

The fisheries and tuna conferences hadn't done much to save her subject matter from extinction, not for lack of trying. What's the point? She didn't want to cross the line into advocacy. She was a scientist not an environmental evangelist.

She noticed that Dr. Jenkins had stopped listening and was running numbers in his head and muttering to himself. He then spoke quietly under his breath. "I stand corrected, a dozen jumbo jets would be about $4.6 billion dollar's worth of tuna. Did I say 6.4?"

Research-based imposed quotas by poorly funded authorities were no contest to the money that was involved in industrialized fishing, or the sophistication of the fishing equipment, which dwarfed even the finest of scientific research vessels. The research ships were once outfitted with state-of-the-art marine survey instruments, but it was hard to keep them up to date. The mother lode of oceanic grant money had gone to seafloor mineral exploration. And there was no way to enforce regulations even when imposed. To close the fish markets would increase demand. Even that can't save them. Many of the fish were ground up and canned before they ever reached the shore, and were carted off in shipping containers. Many were misidentified by uneducated, indentured deck hands. The prize fish were airlifted from the mother ship and served on fine crystal while they were practically still breathing.

Scientists estimated that 75% of the most highly migratory tuna species in the world ocean were caught by enormous nets that sifted the oceans like the pool filter, 10% were caught by 60-mile long lines, 7% by pole and line, and another 8% was a margin of error, or fish caught by other means including fish magnets. None of this included the vast unreported fish catches.

Purse-seine fisheries often target juvenile Pacific bluefin, and the drift gillnet fishery often catch bluefin when fishing for swordfish. Though sport fishing is traditionally less devastating, at times throughout history the number of juveniles killed by recreational fishing exceed that of international commercial operations. Before Mexico established its exclusive economic zone (EEZ) in the late 70s, the U.S. had a large commercial Pacific bluefin purse-seine fishery operating off Baja California and the sport fishing businesses out of San Diego were making a killing.

More recently, unofficial sources reported that juveniles were being caught and confined to unregulated breeding pens in the Baja where their destiny was uncertain. The best guess was there were under 40,000 Pacific bluefin left, and many were moms on their way to spawn who had not yet reproduced, while others were too young, or over the hill.

Fishing companies had no reason to report their catch, share their techniques, or reveal their locations. The floating canneries ground them up and canned them in the privacy of their bilges. Natalie had looked at the bycatch records hoping for more clues. Bycatch was the term used for all the species caught by accident in the nets and hooked by mistake. Even those operations with good intentions couldn't save the bycatch, which usually drowned before they were brought in. There was no way to estimate how many turtles, sharks, dolphins, and mammals were thrown back as dead. These poor innocent creatures were sunk to the bottom in weighted nets before the environmentalists got to them. It was a sad state of affairs but not the job of a scientist to be emotional. Or worse, moralistic.

Dr. Jenkins was studying Natalie's face. She continued. "According to catch data, 85% of all tuna caught were juveniles and thrown back before entering controlled ports. That would offer some hope for population growth but where are they?"

She was obviously exasperated. "So, I'm blaming it on a dramatic shift in ocean circulation that has blown our data collection techniques right out of the water. There is no signal, Dr. Jenkins. Maybe they're traveling so deep they aren't getting picked up by our sensors. Maybe every fish in the food chain is traveling on new highways and byways down there. Byways that we don't have a read on. It's like a new traffic pattern that happened very, very quickly. Which supports what the climate scientists report."

She knew she was right about the climate shift, and that the slightest shifts in the planet's temperature, wind patterns, and atmospheric chemistry were magnified beneath the sea. The recent rise in temperature of the Earth's atmosphere was scientifically proven, though no industry and no country would own up to causing the problem. More carbon was being burned than ever and the sea was absorbing it. The canary in the coalmine was the visible disappearance of healthy coral reefs. The acidity increase was weakened the skeletal structure of coral and fish alike.

The 1950's and 60's will be looked upon in history as the turning point for the oceans and the atmosphere. The age of carbon, methane and mercury emissions, and other pollution. When fishing got taken over by big business technology and became a multi-billion dollar industry. The Earth got poor at the hands of a few greedy billionaires who got rich for short-term gain. Lots of big houses, yachts, jewelry and trust funds. Man had extracted more resources from the planet than could ever be replaced.

Though it was coined as the Age of Flower Power and love, for the ocean it was more like the Age of Stupid and greed.

Dr. Jenkins was lost in thought again. "Well, when all the fish are really gone, at least we won't have to worry about mercury poisoning. The coal burning power plants have created a soup of mercury in our ocean. Fish concentrate toxics in their fat. Mercury levels in fish are 600% over safety levels. There are scientists tracing this to low IQ, and even autism. My wife will be glad to know she's not the only one who has to give up fish. Dana is pregnant you know."

Natalie was stunned in disbelief at how lightly he was treating the dire seriousness of the subject matter. Yet, she forced a polite reply. "Congratulations, Dr. Jenkins. What will you name him or her?"

"Him. His name is one thing we haven't agreed upon yet. We do agree that mercury content in fish and in our bodies is off the charts and Dana won't touch a fish with a 10-foot pole. But I digress. You are stuck in what we call the PhD thesis valley of death. If we can get you through this, you will become the great scientist you are destined to be. You are my star pupil, Natalie. Write up your hypothesis. We'll go to the conference and then come back and tell the advisory board about your dilemma. Few things are pure science anymore. Politics, greed and treachery are factors. As scientists, we must fight the urge to prove theories that we want to believe in. Ask Copernicus. He had to stop believing the world was flat before he could move on. You've got to stop thinking you already have the right answer before you can look for a new one."

With the sun brightly shining overhead, the deep lines etched into Dr. Jenkins's brow looked more pronounced. They drew an expression of perpetual curiosity on his face. Of a man discovering things about the Earth around him with childlike marvel and deep concern. "How many people know that the tagged samples have disappeared?" he asked Natalie. "Heck, maybe the damn tuna have figured out a way to bite each other's tags off! Either that, or there is foul play. I agree that the oceans are dramatically recirculating in response to climate change, but I'm not sure that's your answer. Not yet, anyway. The citizens of this planet have no jurisdiction over the high seas, which should be a protected commons. The governments aren't much help. There is no 911 to call, so it's not so easy to figure out. Big corporations driven by the stock exchange and run by billionaires are paying off politicians to make sure of that!"

They both stared out into the wild blue yonder as if trying to penetrate the surface. It was a touching moment. She was glad she hadn't cancelled the meeting.

Dr. Jenkins broke the silence again. "It's no longer a matter of profiling these wonderful, elusive creatures that have inhabited this planet for 65 million years longer than we have. It's a matter of finding them or finding out what's happened to them. That's the task at hand. It sounds so preposterous I can see why you're caving in."

Natalie felt like the world had lifted off her shoulders a little bit. Temporarily anyway. "I just need some sleep. I stayed up all night preparing for what I was going to report to you today, and to my other advisors on Monday."

Jenkins kept a stern tone. Sympathy had no place here. "Well now you have two more weeks. You are right to take it seriously. There's no consolation prize here at the Center. So, you'd better get everything out on the table, and the sooner the better. The university is not going to give you another extension past this semester without requiring those refresher courses. Good old Betty up in administration will make sure of it. I've already advocated for you, and lost, but I'll try again. Sometimes I think she gets a commission on tuition for prolonging graduations. And if the government has anything to say about it, we can forget about any substantial grant money for anything but local artisan fisheries. They're putting the Food Chain Group on the butcher block. Before you know it, we'll all be scrambling after military money. If we were looking for submarines you could line your office in gold. Lost fish? Not on your life. We'll all be living on peanut butter sandwiches before the general public realizes the fish are all gone."

There was another long pause as they contemplated the future of life as we know it. The Earth would be around a long time, but man might be on a suicide mission. The silence became increasingly uncomfortable… like an eight ball on the pool table, teeter tottering on the edge of the pocket. As though the slightest air current might blow it one way or another, deciding the fate of the game.

"You just keep your eye on the prize, and I'll talk with the board. How do you think it will look if I have a graduate student who doesn't graduate? By the way, have you given life after grad school any thought?"

"No." Her voice cracked. "Not really," she struggled.

Dr. Jenkins could see this was no time to talk about life after grad school The girl was focused on five things. The signatures. "Now, go home and get some sleep for gosh sakes. You are a terrific scientist. Don't get weak in the knees as you're running for the finish line. We want you to graduate!"

Natalie sighed. "Ok, so I have until March 7th right? I'll have it figured out by then."

"Yes, and you'll get back to me about conference, right? The flight to Paris is Saturday and you'll be back by Wednesday. This is how I'm getting your extension approved. Trust me on this one. Oui?"

"Oui, para les pisces," said Natalie, practicing her French.

To clear her head, she took the scenic route home over Mt. Soledad. The coast of southern California stretched south in the distance like a silver ribbon, beyond San Diego Harbor down Imperial Beach and on to Tijuana. Twenty minutes later Natalie walked into her apartment to find a man asleep on the couch and Debbie buried deeply in her bed. Slipping quietly into her room, she set the alarm in time to leave for Friends of the River, sank into the mattress, and zonked out.

CHAPTER SEVEN
Rio de Janeiro
February 14, 5 pm

The rocky granite peaks and valleys of downtown Rio de Janeiro support an eclectic collection of architecture in creative shapes and sizes, giving the cityscape its exotic character. One of Rio's more impressive skyscrapers housed Ocean Enterprises, Inc. on the 58th floor.

From the floor to ceiling glass offices of Ocean Enterprises, Inc., you could almost see forever. Guanabara Bay opened to the Southern Atlantic Ocean where 6,000 miles east lay the submerged Mid-Atlantic Ridge. The submarine mountain range is the longest on Earth. The ridge runs up the middle of the Atlantic Ocean until it breaches the sea surface as Iceland. Its seamounts are taller than Mt. Everest and the valleys deeper than the Grand Canyon. Frigid currents from Antarctica flow north along its western slopes in icy rivers five miles below sea level or *see level* beneath which all is invisible to the naked eye.

Salvador Rodriquez Domingo had built Ocean Enterprises from scratch, starting with his grandfather's small fleet of local fishing boats. Now, the ocean was his oyster, and the high seas were his domain and he was willing to fight for his supremacy.

He was a fit man with good features and a deep sienna face that was clean-shaven and well preserved. He was dressed in a deep navy blue Armani suit and tie in contrast to a bright white starched shirt, which set off the whites of his darting black eyes and his shiny bleached teeth that flashed when he spoke. His thick midnight black hair was combed back in a corduroy pattern.

The man was obviously furious. His eyebrows leapt up and down like as if at battle with the person on the other end of the phone. He was pacing and bobbing his head up and down, then right and left. Holding the receiver as far away from his mouth as possible so could yell as loud as his vocal chords would allow, Salvador put every muscle of his body into hollering at the boat captain who worked for him who as on the other end of the line. A strand of hair shook loose and was bouncing around like a slinky against his brow. He gestured wildly with his free hand that glittered with rings and a diamond-studded vanity watch casting prisms on the very high ceiling. Stretching the phone cord to its limits, he stomped back and forth, slapping the window and finger-combing his hair. The hand that clenched the phone made an exasperating sweep across the seascape beyond.

"Well, just get another helicopter, gawd-dammit," he bellowed. "Get two. Tres! Get a whole pissin' army of them for all I care! Now listen to me, and you listen good. I am putting you in touch with a high definition sonar equipment dealer who has the technology to find a freakin' minnow in the middle of the friggin' high seas. A needle in a haystack!"

"A needlefish on a seamount," the captain interrupted.

"What are you freakin' talking freakin' about?" screamed Salvador with an exasperated sweep of his arm.

“It was a joke. The maritime version of needle in a haystack is needlefish on a seamount.”

“A joke? You’re telling freakin’ jokes while my business is going under?”

A chuckle came over the phone and you could hear some guys in the background joining in the merriment. “That’s funny, too. Fishing business going under. You’re a very funny many Mr. Domingo. Talk to me like that again and you’d better watch your back, uh, your stern.” Like a laugh track in a sitcom, the chuckles in the background presumably from the boat crew came back followed by a burst of belly laughter.

Salvador lowered his voice to a full-force whisper, which caused his mouth to contort. “Look, order those helicopters, and get back to me about that high definition VCD-3DC laser system. I want to know every freakin’ tagged tuna out there on a first name basis.“

“I thought you said *sonar*? Mr. Domingo. Now you say you want a *laser-based* system? My men have already negotiated with the Russians for the laser…"

Domingo cut him off, losing his temper again. "I don't care if it's freakin' SONAR… or LASER… it can be freakin' NUCLEAR for all I care. Just tell me how soon and how much… Got it? Hire a systems specialist to train every idiot on the boat. At sea, gawd dammit. This isn't going to be a port stop for you and your horny crew. They're not leaving that boat until we find every friggin' fish. When you do, I'll put the whole crew up at the freakin' Copa freakin' Cabana freakin' Palace for all I care. And turn off the gawd dam AIS for christ sake. The last thing we need is the global fish watch on our tail." He slammed the phone down, raking the loose strands of hair back to the top of his head.

Salvador struck the intercom button on his desk with his fist while he flipped through the VCD-3DC fish tag finder signal tracking systems brochure. He knew that turning off the Assistance Information System, or AIS, was risky. These signals were monitored by satellite. A vessel that suddenly turned it off would attract global attention. With the help of Google and the Silicon Valley technology nerds, the environmentalists were on the lookout for anything that looked like suspicious illegal, unreported and unregulated fishing, known as IUU. They were developing technology to identify the patterns of vessels that didn't travel a straight line in shipping lanes. It was safer to just turn the bloody AIS off, and he knew it. Especially at night. He tore through the VDC-3D brochure with rage, then ripped it into pieces and threw the bits into the air. They were fluttering to the floor like new fallen snow when a receptionist walked in. Only she wasn't a receptionist. She was his daughter who was filling in for his receptionist as part of her intern program.

She arrived in style, perfectly coifed in a creatively designed business suit that afforded a 320° view of her full breasts, and her bare midriff. Matching the jacket was a pair of hot pants belted by a gold chain which matched the heavy collection that hung from her wrists and her neck, which matched her dangling earrings. This girl could sink a ship. From out of the hot pants, thundered some very hardy thighs that teeter tottered on her 6" heels. The heels brought her height to nearly six feet. Salvador's face softened when she came clanging and clicking into the room. She kissed both cheeks of her father, enveloping him in such strong perfume that he coughed.

"What do we have we here?" she signed, seeing the paper bits floating through the air to the floor. "A snowstorm in Rio? Tut-tut. You'll have a stroke. Now, what can I do for you?" said V, short for Veronica Maria Guadalupe Domingo.

He dropped his voice into an exaggerated robot-like monotone, dramatically enunciating every single syllable. "Kindly get these people on the phone please V," he said picking up the remains of the product brochure from the floor. "Please ask them if their instruments can pick up a signal on tagged m-i-g-r-a-t-o-r-y, p-e-l-a-g-i-c fish, if it's not too much to ask. I'd like to know how deep and for how long? How deep and for how long? Could you do that for me?"

“No problem, I’ll get back to you right away. Anything else?” V answered her father in her most cheerful yet professional tone, which mocked his by its pure contrast. Salvador smiled at his daughter. “That’s all. Thank you.”

As Veronica went clanging and clicking out of the room, he followed her. “You’re a smart girl, V. You passed physics, anyway. Maybe you can ask them if they do product development for private clients. We are interested in developing an anti-signal system that voids out tag signals on certain occasions. And voids out AIS signals, too. Your father is a very smart man.”

In minutes V was back. “Your real receptionist has returned from lunch and wants her space back,” said V, rolling her eyes. “So, I’ll just work in here,” she chirped with sarcastic cheeriness. She carried scotch tape and the pieces of the torn brochure of spy technology for the undersea environment over to the windowsill. While humming an anonymous tune, she laid the pieces out along the sill like a jigsaw puzzle and got to work. When she found matching pieces, she squealed with delight and taped them together on the window.

"Want a drink?" her dad offered, opening his bar cabinet. "You're old enough now, right?" he said with slight hesitation. "Anyway, in this business you need it!"

"Why, yes, I'd love a drink," she said in a cocky grown up voice. "And please hand me the phone." He handed her the phone and busied himself at the bar. V began flirting into the receiver with tech support at SeaMee, Inc., in a voice meant for her father to hear. "The b5600 can see everything? Even juveniles? I see. The GPS point is an extra feature? That's fine." With this, her dad nodded and toasted her from across the room with a shot of tequila and slugged it down. Then he poured one for her, and another for him. She winked in his direction and remained fully engrossed in her conversation with tech support.

Salvador was impressed by the mastery his daughter had acquired over commercial fishing industry jargon. It runs in the family, he thought. He'd been the same way at her age. Times had changed since his great grandfather started the business. But the hunger for tuna, the chicken of the sea, had not. There was a veracious appetite for large wiggling bluefin tuna, especially among the Japanese elite. He was cornering the market and beating them at their own game.

CHAPTER EIGHT
A Hotel in Paris
February 14, 10 am

The quaint streets of Paris that ran adjacent to the River Seine were covered in a delicate veil of fresh snow. It clung like fine lace curtains to the beveled glass windows of the Hotel de Lycee, which glowed from the parlor lamps within. A fortyish woman wearing a doily-collared dress was working the front desk of the hotel lobby, which was well appointed with antiques. Even the *bring! bring!* of the hotel's telephone was a flashback in time. Antoinette, the receptionist, pushed some paperwork and a faux quill pen across the counter to an arriving guest as she answered the phone. "Hotel de Lycee," she said in a cheery tone.

Salvador Rodriguez Domingo spoke on the other end of the line from Rio in a soft, seductive voice. He sat alone in his office now as the sun sank behind the jagged backdrop of the Serra da Mantiqueira to the west, while the ocean went dark to the east but for the pins of light that were vessels at sea. Dusk settled over the city.

The twinkle of the quiet evening would soon give way to Rio's flashy nightlife of strobe lights and the boom of Latin music. Salvador was feeling good. "Hello my French sex kitten, is it still Valentine's Day in Paris? Or am I too late to tell my love that you are the air that I breathe, without which I would choke to my death?"

Antoinette's ashen face blushed rose in the cheeks and she turned away from the guest who was checking in. "Domingo, it's you. When are you coming to Paris?" she whispered.

"I hope to attend the International Tuna Conference in Paris later this week. Can you hold me a reservation on February 17th for three nights? Or," he said even more softly, "should I stay for four?"

Cheeks burning, she slid the hotel guests an envelope with their key and pointed them to the stairs. Her heart was beating hard when she turned back to the phone with a giggle that seemed out of character. "How about you stay here for the rest of your life? Remember we were talking about that?"

"Yes, and I remember exactly what you were wearing at the time." He paused to reflect her timid body spread before him, pale against the French linen. He loved her shy demure in contrast to the ballsy chicks he bagged in Rio. It's too bad this conversation had turned so quickly to this topic because it always led them right back to the same place. Why he couldn't marry her. His voice became disciplinary. "And I also remember explaining very clearly to you, my sweet Antoinette, why that is impossible right now. You must try to live in the moment. How do you say it? C'est la vie? So, be a doll baby and reserve me Room 52 for February 17, 18 and 19. Would you like me to read you my credit card number?"

Antoinette, who had no other lover, was miffed. "Okay, I have you booked for three nights, Mr. Domingo, *sir*. And don't worry about your credit card number. I already have it!" She hung up. And I just might *use* it, she thought sinking into her victim mode.

CHAPTER NINE
February 14, 4 pm
Natalie and Debby, in Debby's car

Natalie and Debby were singing out loud to the soundtrack from "Mama Mia" as they drove up the windy mountain roads to Cuyamaca Rancho State Park, east of San Diego, to the Friends of the River meeting. They turned at a sign to the ranger station. The road crossed a bridge that spanned a deep ravine through which a small waterfall of melting snow from the mountain peaks cascaded and fell into a natural pool that spilled over into a stream that gurgled on down the canyon on its way to the coast. The ranger station was home to the club's monthly potluck.

The conversation inside the car had turned to Chad again, like it always did. Debby was patient with her friend but forever looking for any opportunity to change the topic. Maybe if Natalie talked about the break up over and over again enough she would exhaust herself and move on. Or maybe being a good listener just made it worse by egging her on. She didn't know. Debby was adamant, however, about pulling Natalie out of her slump. She'd known the pre-Chad Natalie and was convinced that the happy-go-lucky babe she once knew lurked somewhere beneath the pain. A happy tune would someday play again in her mind where now there was a scratchy needle playing a broken record of woulda, coulda, shoulda in the poor girl's beautiful head. She resented Chad for that. Guys were literally having fistfights over Natalie back in high school. It was Chad's aloofness that had attracted her. He was a pretty-girl collector. A connoisseur who took pride in his ability to identify and capture a nice piece of ass. There was Miss California, a newscaster, a swimsuit model, Natalie, and then a photographer. Something must have happened to him as a boy. Maybe he was potty trained too early or weaned too long. Maybe his mom neglected him, sentencing him to a life of chasing down female affection. Perhaps a narcissist? She read somewhere that narcissists are mentally sculpted by a consistent drum beat of criticism during childhood.

An astute purveyor of knowledge and understanding, Natalie had read every book on every type of dysfunction and disorder in the library looking for clues on how to love him better, and make him happier. The one on narcissism gave specific instructions in the summary at the end to run like the wind and do not look back as these mow down anything in their path with no remorse. But, as Debby knew, Natalie didn't take failure well. She wanted to fix him. Not only that, she lived in fear that she'd made a wrong, irreversible decision in her life. She couldn't come to terms with it. From beneath the rubble of her friend's broken dream, Debby was convinced that Natalie would rise again.

"Anyway, Nat," she said. "Even if you were still married, what makes you think Chad would be coming to your rescue right now? The guy can hardly spell his own name, let alone help write a PhD."

Mentioning Chad's shortfalls was a very touchy mental mine field. If you took it too far Natalie would rush to his defense. Everyone close to Natalie these days was stuck in the balancing act of slightly dissing Chad, but not enough to cause her to rise with a sword and take his side, which is exactly what she was doing now. "He gave me moral support. That was one thing about Chad. When it came to my career he was always there for me," she said, driving Debby totally berserk.

"There for YOU?" Debby retorted in her best you-must-be-crazy tone like it was the most outlandish thing that she'd ever heard. Like someone had just told her the moon was made of feta. "Excuse me. He was there for your career for HIM!"

Natalie scrunched up her face trying to comprehend the meaning of him being there for her, for him. Debby clarified, "He got his marine tech job because of your status in the marine biology department in the food chain group. You were higher up the food chain, in fact. You got him that job. You're the star of the show, babe."

"But, I wanted *him* to be the star of the show. That was the whole point. Guys need that. Anyway, I don't feel like much of a star now. More like a meteorite making a crash landing." She made a fizzle sound that spiraled and imploded on impact. "That's what wiped out the dinosaurs you know."

Thank gawd, thought Debby. She'd moved onto a new topic. Dinosaurs. Debby seized this opportunity to change the direction of the conversation. Halleluiah! "Is that what happened to the dinosaurs, Nat? Tell me more. When exactly was that?" By and by, after a very nice chat about the Yucatan Peninsula where the meteorite supposedly landed, and where they'd also spent some stupendous spring breaks together, they pulled up to the ranger station which was a log cabin in the pines on the edge of a precipice over the deeply scoured ravine.

Natalie turned the car off and Debby rummaged around in her purse, pulling out a lipstick, blush and powder puff. She turned to Natalie. "Nat, look at me." Despite the hell she was going through, she hadn't fully lost her sweet look of wonder and innocence. It was a cross between a deer staring in the headlights and childlike curiosity. Her eyes were such a deep dark blue that you could hardly see the pupils, and that added an element of mystery to her face. Whatever it was, guys fell for her usually in a matter of seconds. “Pucker,” said Debby. Natalie obliged, and her friend applied faun colored lipstick and mussed up her hair a little to give her friend a more approachable, slightly unruly look. That her body was perfect and her voice melodic was an unfair distribution of wealth. That she was oblivious to her beauty had caused her to make some poor decisions when it came to men.

Inside the ranger station, a poster on the wall had a picture of a lake morphed into a hamburger that read, “It takes 100 gallons of water to make one hamburger.” On the back deck, which hung out over the ravine, a crowd of athletic coeds was gathered around a keg sharing their most life-threatening heroic experiences on the rivers of the world. The air smelled like pine needles and beer.

With few rivers left undammed in California, the whitewater crowd was often at the mercy of the water authorities which decided when to open the dams, and by how much. The dams were controversial, and the Friends of the River had fought long and hard to prevent many of them. Some of the discounted water rights had been grandfathered into gentleman "vanity farms" of wealthy celebrities, as tax write-offs, and they had to use it or lose it. Some grew useless crops and paid a fraction of the price that residents paid for drinking water. The dams allowed them to indulge their hobbies. Other farmers were legitimately supplying the majority of the nation's fruits, vegetables and nuts.

The dams in particular were built on the premise that California was an arid state and all the water had to be captured. This premise often disregarded the rights to the water by communities downstream and it was complicated. Environmental groups claimed that some of these water diversions were not necessary, and thus neither were the dams. If archeologists hadn't found artifacts on the banks of some of the rivers and listed the basins as heritage sites, there would be more dams. But many officials were still pushing for more water storage because of the drought and flooding effects of climate warming. Also, they'd get federal funds to build them, which meant jobs and that meant votes. Storing water was important to prepare for the unknown and sporadic weather of the south-west. But how and at what cost? The more militant global environmental groups called it the "Dam Scam," and were literally blowing dams up on major rivers throughout the world.

To further compound the issue, beaches at the deltas of these rivers no longer got the sediment deposits they were due, and were eroding. This caused all kinds of complex political havoc, which was becoming known as the great sand wars. Though engineers would be more than happy to scoop the sand from behind the dams and truck it to the beaches, it was contaminated from agricultural pesticides. Beaches down current from river mouths were no longer nourished with sand. Houses were slipping into the ocean as waves chipped away at the cliffs upon which they were built. The buffer zone of sand was disappearing rapidly. Tourists who sought wide sandy beaches to lie on were disappearing too. In some places, surfers could no longer enjoy the long wave breaks that southern California was so famous for. In other places the waves got better, deflected by man-made jetties constructed to accumulate sediment. Nothing is easy when you mess with nature.

Yet, with people flocking to arid southern California with a local geology that could store very little ground water, water officials were playing it safe. New technologies were in the works to save more, store more, leak less, desalinate, and level the playing field.

Despite the droughts and the politics, the Friends of the River didn't complain about the spectacular gush of whitewater released when the dams were opened in spring when they reached their capacity from the melting snow.

The silver lining was that when they let out the dams, riding the river over the terrain below was the absolute thrill of a lifetime. The Disneyland log ride had nothing on this one. Some of the rapids were Class 7. That's what the Friends of the River were hoping for over Memorial Day weekend.

At the meeting at the ranger station, Friends of the River were crowded on the deck around the keg and talking. Conversations were full of enthusiasm, speculation and activism. "It looks like it's going to be a Class 6." And, "When the packed powder at Mammoth melts, it's going to be like Niagara friggin' Falls up north." And, "Let's blow the whole dam thing up!" And, "So, what time exactly is the dutch boy pulling his thumb out of the dike this year?" By now, Debby had sidled up to a well-built guy wearing nothing but bike pants. She was giving him a hip bump saying, "Oh, you ski, too? So do I!" Natalie overheard this and was amused by how quickly her friend could make friends. It lifted her spirits. Gotta love her, thought Natalie. She'd been skiing with Debby. It took one hour and forty-five minutes to get her down the bunny slope at Big Bear Mountain, and she had complained the whole time about why Maybelline would call their mascara waterproof, when it was running all down her face.

Getting more and more boisterous, the Friends of the River began to make toasts. They raised their beers to whitewater, the river, to explosives, and to Natalie, the chairwoman of the Spring whitewater trip.

A familiar voice cut through the clamor of voices. "Are we talking kayaks, canoes, rafts, or hey, how about surfboards?" The sound of Chad's voice shocked her neurological system and Natalie spilled her beer all down her t-shirt. Under her breathe, but a little too loud, she heard Debby say, "How about in a barrel?" Chad heard this and snuck up behind Natalie and put his arm around her shoulders right in front of everybody. Horrified, Natalie jerked away. To which Chad responded, "You know, Nat, that's your problem. Anger management."

Natalie's psychological needle was approaching what her yoga instructor called the *red zone*, It took every ounce of will in Natalie's psyche not to shove him over the railing despite being typically mild-mannered. She turned to Debby. "Let's go." As if on autopilot, they both headed straight for the car. "Just keep walking, don't turn around," Debby told her. Once they were in full flight down the stairs, Natalie asked the inevitable question, "So, was she the shutterbug with him?"

"I doubt it. Probably not. She would have been all over him once she saw you. And he looked alone," Debby said choosing each word delicately. She was mad as hell that Chad would show up at Friends of the River knowing that Natalie would be there, and how volatile this whole thing was. It was a bonfire of emotions, and Chad had poured the kerosene on it and lit a match. There is common decency in divorce. Split the stuff, and split the friends. These were Natalie's, fair and square.

At the bottom of the steps, Natalie turned to her. "Will you go back and ch… check?" she asked. Her eyelids were flinching and her lips trembling. Debby hated to see her stoop to this level.

Debby knew Natalie well enough that if she didn't go back and find out if that bitch was with him she would never hear the end of it. Obediently, she went back up the stairs to look around for the slut who stole her best friend's husband. She'd be easy to recognize by her plunging neckline and body language. That was her hook. Debby had seen her in action around

Chad, long before Natalie had noticed. She wasn't that surprised that Chad took the bait.

Natalie was hot-footing it down the path to the car with her face buried in her hands when she collided into a guy who was locking his bike to a pine tree. Upon contact, he dropped his bike helmet. It bounced twice before disappearing over the cliff. The look of horror on Natalie's face shocked him more than the sudden loss of his helmet. They both listened to it ricochet a few times, echo through the ravine, and then stop. Silence dangled in the air for a moment as they exchanged looks. "It's just a helmet," he said calmly, using his hands to accentuate the notion of remaining even-keeled. "Just a helmet." Natalie's eyes followed the path that the helmet had taken. She crept to the drop-off and peered below to discover that it had landed on a ledge about 45 feet down the cliff. "I'm so sorry," said Natalie, gasping for air and fighting back tears.

Wow, this girl was taking her folly pretty hard. He winked an eye, and held up his forefinger to indicate that he had an idea. Pulling some rope from his backpack, he knotted it around a tree and repelled down the ravine and back. He was back with the helmet in a matter of a minute.

"You can stop holding your breath now," he said. "It's ok. See?"

He put it on his head, snapped it, and grinned. Something about the girl looked so distressed and fragile, he had an urge to comfort her. To tell her that everything was going to be all right now. She was pretty, but more than that she looked terribly vulnerable. Like she bore the weight of world on her shoulders in earnest. It was an uncanny combination he'd only seen once before. Alice in Wonderland he thought.

"Hello miss, uh, ma'am. I'm Jamie Robertson," he said, extending his hand. "United States Coast Guard." Natalie remained despondent. She just stood there, with her mind still on Chad. He thought he'd try something else. "Excuse me, is this where the Friends of the River meeting is? Why were you leaving? Is the meeting over?" He pulled Tupperware out of his pack. "Darn, I brought a casserole and everything."

"No! The meeting hasn't really started yet. Please, go. I'm just waiting for my…" Where the hell was Debby? It must have been fifteen minutes by now. She finished her sentence. "My friend."

Something seemed oddly sad about this adorable gal. He made a note of this and excused himself politely before her *friend* showed up. Biking up the mountain had tuckered him out and he was in no mood for confrontation with some jealous boyfriend.

Natalie just stood there encased in a bubble of emotion and feeling pathetic. The Friends of the River was her gang, not Chad's. She brought him here. Why couldn't he just stay away from her and go hang out in Encinitas with his surfer dudes. Hell, when they were married that's all he wanted to do. What's the sudden interest in the Friends of the River? He couldn't stand these *river wonks* as he called them.

As she watched the Coast Guard guy go up the stairs, she got the childish idea to flirt with him and flaunt him in front of Chad. “Wait for me!” she called, following him up the steps as his mind churned to find an inroad to a conversation. “So, wow, that must have been quite a ride up here. It’s a little far inland for the Coast Guard. What does our red, white and blue have to do with Friends of the River?”

Her tone had changed so quickly, it made him nervous and put him on military alert. “Yes m’am. I’m off duty, ma’am,” he said.

Natalie just stood there at the door trying to think of ways to keep the conversation going so it would look like they were together. My name in Natalie Scott,” she said in a hushed tone so as not to be overheard, revealing that they didn’t know each other. She managed a smile. “So, what brings you here?”

“My colleagues from California State Fish and Wildlife invited me. To be honest, I’d prefer the Colorado River run through Grand Canyon but this will do while I’m stationed in San Diego.

I'll make do with man-made whitewater. These dams have turned southern California into a real theme park."

"Ma'am," he continued. "I don't want to get personal, but is something bothering you?" At this point Natalie was practically blocking the door. Just what she needed. A shrink. "So, you're a therapist, too?" she asked. The embarrassment on his face made her feel terrible for acting sarcastic. He looked like a puppy that had been kicked across the floor. As if on cue they both said, "I'm so sorry."

Jamie had no clue what to do next. Girls, he thought. A total mystery.

Then Debby appeared. Her glassy eyes hinted that she might have snuck in a beer or two during her reconnaissance trip. "As I suspected, he's alone," she said before noticing the Coast Guard guy with the Tupperware.

Jamie Robertson had regained his composure and was now amused by the whole scene, and had become slightly charmed by these girls. Had he been at sea too long, or were these the cutest girls he'd seen since high school prom?

Like a moth to a flame, a part of Natalie wanted to keep up the dialogue long enough to walk into the meeting together, laughing and flirting just to make Chad jealous and let him know she was over him. The other part told her to flee. That part won out.

She turned to Debby. "We can still make it downtown for happy hour," she said to Debby, who beamed with joy at the suggestion. "That's the spirit! I'm so proud of you—the road to recovery. Stay in the light."

Natalie turned to Jamie, who stood there bewildered. Suddenly she remembered the brownies she had brought that were still in her bag. "Sorry… again. Here, take these!" Then she bounded down the stairs again, racing toward the car. Leave it to Debby to linger behind, leaving no man un-flirted. From the car, Natalie beeped the horn, mortified by the whole situation.

On the drive back down the mountain, Debby was bubbling with excitement. “Do you know what he said?”

“Who? What who said?”

“That wicked hunk, you nerd. You know for a scientist you’re not that smart.”

“Thanks for the vote of confidence.”

“He asked me why you were so upset.”

“What did you say?”

“I told him about Chad, and his dumb anger-management comment.”

“What did he say?”

“He asked me exactly what Chad looked like and watched you get in the car, with this sort of twinkle in his eye.”

“You lie.”

They rounded a bend and the lights of San Diego gleamed in the distance against a hot pink sunset that was mirrored by the San Diego Harbor.

CHAPTER TEN
Marine Biology Department
February 15, 5 pm

Maybe it was the margaritas, but after she got home from happy hour the night before, Natalie had thrown caution to the wind and emailed her advisors to invite them to a closed session despite having cancelled a more formal presentation of her preliminary thesis. Natalie had personally invited several key advisors and a small group of scientists in her inner circle to discuss her dilemma.

She was setting up her projector in the conference room when Jim Saltonstahl, her advisor from National Oceanic and Atmospheric Administration (NOAA) and professor emeritus, snuck in behind her and sat down in the first row. The rustle of papers as he rummaged through his briefcase scared the wits out of her. "Salt!" she exclaimed, calling him by his nickname. "What a surprise! You're early."

"Jumpy nerves?" Salt asked.

"Just a little. Thank you for coming."

Captain James Saltonstahl had been with NOAA for nearly 30 years and was facing retirement. He had served in the U.S. Navy on a ship looking for subs and then landed a job at NOAA as the captain of a research vessel that was running transects across the ocean floor with a bathymetry sounder to record the terrain. The data became some of the earliest used to map the ocean floor, building on the earlier work of Maria Tharp and others.

He was also among the first to develop tracking methods to study and monitor the ocean's fish populations. Back then the sonar equipment picked up the signal of fish schools as shadows in the water column. This data was deciphered by graduate students to distinguish among fish species as best they could, as well as whales and dolphins. As the industrial revolution turned the ocean into man's dumping ground, the same equipment was also used to track trash and debris. These data collections catapulted Salt to the top of the scientific community as each new study credited him for the original data. Now he held a top position at NOAA and had been awarded an honorary doctorate. Salt commanded the respect of everyone in the field. His simpatico for Greenpeace had won over the hearts of environmentalists but created some controversy among the right wing. That was a sacrifice he was willing to make. He'd seen dramatic changes in the world oceans in his day, from plastic pollution to overfishing, to the destruction of coral reefs.

Having been a Navy man who once hunted Russian submarines, overfishing was now his pet peeve. The players in the industrialized fishing industry were the ocean's modern day public enemy. They were pirates, thugs and crooks, who were robbing the small island countries of their fish, their eco-tourism and their livelihoods. Their unbridled, unregulated operations in areas beyond national jurisdiction (ABNJ) were filtering every living thing out of the sea with purse seiners the size of Manhattan. Huge trawlers that dragged and combed the seafloor in wide tracks were mowing down everything in their path. It was the worst invasion in human history and Salt knew it. Natalie was lucky to have him on her committee, but you couldn't pull the wool over his eyes.

“How are you?” Natalie asked him.

“Well, I’ve been living on coffee and donuts in the marine conference circuit. Speaking of which, Dr. Jenkins informs me you are coming to ITC to show the world that we’ve got young blood working with us. That we’re not just a bunch of old government farts waiting to retire into cushy consulting jobs."

"Well, I wouldn't want that," laughed Natalie, feeling better from the therapeutic effects of laughter. Seeing her smile prompted him to go on.

"We've also been getting a lot of heat lately about government employees going over to the dark side. Last month a contractor got caught cooking the books with bogus surveys, and ratcheting up the bills. He was fudging fish surveys to make a quick buck. A retired fisheries guy, no less. Go figure. Treachery is everywhere. He knew perfectly well that we use those numbers to determine catch quotas."

Natalie still hadn't committed to Dr. Jenkin's ITC invitation and tried to change the subject. "So what's the word out there on the high seas?"

"Twenty hours of fish quota discussions with no resolution. Boats switching flags doubling up on quotas, refusing to provide data, making up data, changing vessel numbers, you name it. We need to raise funds to monitor the black market trade in fish markets with honest custom officers, who can't be bought off. Well, enough about that. It's show time! Are you ready?" Saltonstahl's attention got diverted to the other advisors who began to file into the lab.

Seeing that every single one of her advisors had shown up, some uninvited, even though she had officially cancelled her talk reminded her of the gravity of her research. She had forgotten the importance of her work and had focused on her failings. This was her moment to step up to the plate. Yet, the prospect of ridicule by the esteemed audience made her heart pound so hard, her eardrums hurt from the inside out, leaving her all but deaf. She felt like she was drowning in her own fear. Saltonstahl noticed her distress and stepped up to the podium as her wingman. This helped. He tapped the mike a few times, and she was relieved to detect the amplified tap-tap coming from the speakers. She was alive! Her ears were working.

Salt began. "Let's welcome our soon-to-be, we hope, doctor Natalie Scott. She called us together to present a preliminary assessment of her research titled *"Trends in Bluefin Tuna Populations: Theories on Population Density."*

Natalie could literally feel the artery leading up through her spinal cord to her head, which was pulsating. For a moment she was back in fourth grade at the Spelling Bee Championship being asked to spell dichotomy. From somewhere deep in her sub consciousness, a surge of self-confidence fueled by adrenaline saved her. She began to hear her own voice coming through the speakers.

"As you know my final thesis dissertation and submission is due in two months. You may be aware that I cancelled my public lecture today. I felt I should talk with some of you in confidence here in the lab to put some scientific incongruities in my thesis defense on the table. Shortcomings in the data, to be specific."

Now, breathe she thought. Stop and take a deep breath. These people wanted her to graduate just as much as she did. If she failed, it would reflect on them. Though frankly, they probably wouldn't mind a bit if she had to stick around for another year. Her research had become valuable to the institution and they had the power to make a small post-doc stipend appear if push came to shove. They had already hinted at a post-doctorate position, but that wasn't an option now. She needed to move on.

Think, think, she thought, as they focused their full attention on her.

She suddenly recalled her father's public speaking tip to pause and look people in the eye, one by one if she got stage fright. Natalie looked at each advisor as if they were a firing squad. One by one, she felt like she was staring down the barrel of a gun. She then walked to the blackboard, not too fast, not too slow. This was her show. It was the Spelling Bee she'd aced as a kid. This was her big chance to get the direction she needed from the institution that would approve her final thesis, or not. Better get their feedback sooner than later. She'd made a decision during happy hour to go ahead and present to the advisors alone, informally in the lab. It became obvious after the margaritas that it was the best thing to do. She began to feel confident about her decision. Relieved, actually. She needed their help and there was no time to lose.

At the blackboard, she drew the globe with the major continents and ocean circulation patterns, and then superimposed Pacific bluefin migration routes, which often took these super swimmers right through enemy waters. The narrow straights of Bering Sea, the Sea of Japan, and shipping lanes. Through places where nobody cared about the longevity of the species which has once been revered as holy by ancient civilizations. With the eloquent strokes of an artist, she drew new patterns of deep-sea currents, driven by the cold, dense water from land-locked glaciers melting and entering the ocean at the poles. She drew heavy currents dropping to the seafloor and flowing in clockwise patterns in the northern hemisphere and counter clock-wise patterns in the southern hemisphere, displacing the warmer currents and explained that this was creating a new paradigm for fish migration.

"As many of you know, I have been collecting data from all available sources on large pelagic migratory fish as it pertains specifically to the Pacific bluefin tuna. The sources include: tagging; buoys; government data; fisheries researchers; independent surveys; commercial fishing operations, catch and release figures; canneries, sport fisheries; tournaments; fish markets; shipping points of call; groceries; and delis. Atypical sources included food magazines; dietary organizations, NGOs, environmental groups, census reports, pet food markets, and seafood restaurants around the world to help get a best estimate on bluefin catch and consumption numbers. My data points include species identification, food chain position, maturity and spawning stages, length and weight, mortality estimates, catch data, predictions on losses to bi-catch, temperature anchoring, and GPS coordinates."

She stopped. They probably got the point. She's done the research. Duh. She erased her diagram and picked up the chalk again. In bold strokes she drew a vertical y axis, crossed with a horizontal x axis.

There were no females in the room, but to make a point she included them in her next address. "Ladies and gentlemen, by my calculations, the population of large pelagic, migratory fish, Bluefin, in particular, had become imperceptible to modern tracking technology." At this point she drew her population curve up until the year 1960. The slope maintained a sustainable level. In 1960, it took a downturn. In 1975 it dipped dramatically. In the last two months, it took a nosedive, plunging below zero.

"According to my most recent data, the population is, literally, off the charts. Below the X axis. We are scientists, not environmentalists, and a doctorate thesis is not the place for politics. We are pacifists, not alarmists. But as I struggle to find an explanation for this phenomenon, I cannot. My best hypothesis is that the bluefin are traveling in new patterns, at new depths. They've swum off my radar."

Her audience just stared at the graph. Someone coughed a little bit. Was that a chuckle or a cough?

"I ask that you support my theory that the radical heating of the Earth's atmosphere and sea surface temperatures since the industrial revolution, compounded by an influx of melting ice at the Poles has redirected ocean currents and the last remaining Pacific bluefin have found new, deeper highways and byways and are avoiding detection. Earth's climate is going through radical changes as described in the findings by colleagues in the atmospheric science department. This is a historical shift, with nothing like it recorded in the geologic history for nearly 10,000 years. Our present data on tuna dates back nearly a century."

She continued, running on fear-based adrenalin. "This is a radical change. As you know, the dramatic shift in ocean circulation is set off at the poles where melting ice caps from land glaciers in Greenland and Antarctica in particular, are creating new currents that affect the distribution of food sources. Enormous changes in the salinity, density, depth and direction of the currents in which the large pelagic fish catch a ride have been disturbed. They may be traveling so deep that they are beyond perception of even our most highly sophisticated tracking technology. Yet, the catch figures don't reflect this. Not that I believe much in those."

Salt raised his hand. "But the sales figures of bluefin are up, correct? Historically, commercial fishing fleets simply refuse to acknowledge quotas, local jurisdictions, and country affiliations. They have robbed small islands of their livelihood. The operators have lobbyists in Geneva, Paris, Rio, London, DC, Barcelona, and even at the UN, fighting against protecting spawning areas, establishing marine sanctuaries, and declaring the high seas a global common that need to be governed fairly. I just don't believe the catch data I'm getting. And I don't know where my tags are."

This wasn't going well. She erased the board, and drew another chart. Natalie had purposely not handed out a copy of her graphs. She was a good scientist. She didn't want to print out her data, or email it either. It was not for public consumption yet and she suspected some might not be substantiated.

She drew on the blackboard the mathematical curve of the prediction she had made for bluefin when she first began her research eight years ago. Though she had predicted a decline, the curve leveled off, with 30% of them in early stages of spawning, rather than bottoming out. She superimposed the line of the actual population as represented by her data. It dropped below the X axis. In short, they were pretty much gone. Wiped out. Like the dinosaurs. Caput!

She then used Atlantic bluefin as reference. The Deep Horizon oil spill in the Gulf of Mexico was an important area where the Atlantic population regenerates and the timing couldn't have been worse. Just as the eggs and larvae entered the Gulf to mature, they got coated in oil and then pummeled with toxic dispersants designed to hide the damage. If the oil didn't get them, the dispersants surely did. But, what about the Pacific bluefin? Had something happened?

"I keep thinking that I am missing something here somewhere," Natalie said to her advisors. Then she stopped.

This time, Dr. Jenkins interrupted. "The size of one gill net would cover Manhattan and there are supposedly now 13,000 boats setting these nets, for a total of 12,860 days a year, catching approximately 2.6 billion tons of fish per year. Divide that by an average of 400 pounds, it's a lot of fish. I am beginning to suspect that true figures on illegal bycatch would double that. Still even with the destructive fishing techniques, the population should be regenerating, though not at the rate that Ms. Scott could possibly have predicted."

Natalie's scientific earnestness was evident as she braced herself for questions. Her dark side told her that her advisors would accuse her of slacking off, being lazy. She pushed back negative thinking. Though eight years isn't an unusual time to take getting a PhD, during the last six months since Chad left, she had to admit that she'd lost some her enthusiasm. But, now, her adrenalin was racing and there was no stopping her.

One thing any speaker dreads is a blank look on the faces of an audience when they are asked if there are any questions. She scanned the faces, one at a time. The advisors began talking amongst themselves.

Salt got up and took control of the room. "Well, if there are no further questions for Mrs, uh, Miss… Scott, thank you all for coming. Good day to you," he said blushing from his blunder.

As the scientists filed out of the room, Salt and Jenkins pulled her aside. "I think they got what you were saying. They were just speechless, like scientists get when hit with something so radical," said Salt. Then Jenkins added, "But they concurred that you better figure this out. By the way, here is your plane ticket, your conference badge, and the NOAA booth number."

Salt said, "Please help us man the NOAA booth, or woman it should I say. Maybe you'll get a job offer." He winked.

Ya, she thought. An entry-level job offer for undergrads.

CHAPTER ELEVEN
UC Campus Administration Office
February 19, 4:45 pm

The phone rang at graduate administration on upper campus where students pay their tuition, apply for transfers, and submit their forms and files. Betty Stolz barked a half-hearted *hello.* "Hey Betty, it's Doug Jenkins from Marine Bio. How's life treating you up there?"

Betty had been in graduate administration for twenty-five years and she knew when someone was kissing up to her. Jenkins didn't need to introduce himself. She'd known him since he was a wee grad student desperate to graduate. "I'm fine, Dr. Jenkins, how may I help you today?"

Jenkins had hoped for a warmer reception, but pressed on. "What is the drop dead date when a signed thesis has to be delivered to administration to qualify for spring graduation?"

Betty confirmed that it was Friday, April 30. No exceptions. Signed, sealed and delivered.

Jenkins should have known not to pursue the issue, but he did. "Can you make an exception?"

"Fridays we close early. At 4 pm," she said firmly and hung up.

Jenkins spoke into the dead phone. "Thanks, Betty. Nice talking with you. Always a pleasure!"

Natalie and Dr. Jenkins were in the lab together, strategizing and planning her spring schedule. They'd put Betty on the speakerphone to make sure there was no miscommunication. At least they got the answer they were looking for. There was no wiggle room.

Jenkins thought Natalie needed cheering up. "So there is nothing more for you to do today at this point but head to TG." TG was a grad student watering hole named after TGIF, thank goodness it's Friday, but it opened and closed depending on scientific breakthroughs, graduate thesis defenses, or celebrating a discovery. It was place with popcorn, ping pong, pool tables, sofas, and a keg of beer. The tradition was created to encourage cross communications among different scientific disciplines. The hope was that interdisciplinary discussions among students would foster new breakthroughs and lead to discoveries that put the institute on the map. Mostly they shared complex equations and nerdy jokes. Natalie once brought Debby there. "Those guys have their own language," she had said on her way out. "And I don't speak it."

Jenkins thought TG would be good for Natalie today. "Why don't you discuss your dilemma with some of the other grad students? You're not the first grad student to get cold feet about her findings right at the last minute. There are probably at least a dozen students just like you drinking a beer over at TG right now! I'll walk you over."

As they passed the diving locker in the service lot, they could see old Al, the oldest diver on Earth, fixing regulators and filling tanks. He looked up and greeted them. "Well if it isn't Natalie Scott! Haven't seen you at any Bottom Scratcher meetings, Natalie. We've got a night dive in the San Diego Harbor coming up for the

Fish and Wildlife to look for illegal lobster traps. You coming?"

The Bottom Scratchers is the oldest dive club in America. Only the strongest, bravest and most experienced divers are offered membership. They are seasoned divers available for search and rescue operations, illegal lobster traps recovery, and underwater commercial jobs. Natalie had supplemented her grant stipend with other Bottom Scratchers members by scrubbing the hulls of the research vessels and Navy ships stationed at Point Loma for $100/hour. With battery-powered rotary scrapers, they secured themselves to the hull with a magnetic harness. Little by little, they'd inch their way from bow to stern, up and down, scraping off an accumulation of barnacles and growth of foreign species that the ships had picked up from faraway places on their journeys around the world.

Al was someone who Natalie would sorely miss, if and when she graduated. "Count me in, and let me know the next time there is a hull job. My grant money ran out. I'm running on fumes," she said. Al offered to put in a few calls to the shipyard.

Dr. Jenkins and Natalie kept walking through campus toward TG, where they encountered Spar, a second year grad student in the ocean chemistry department who was studying mercury in fish. They started talking and Spar shared some findings. He estimated that over 240 tons of mercury is released into the air each year in the US alone from combustion of medical waste incineration, municipal waste incineration, and coal-burning power plants. Mercury is absorbed by the sea and collects in fatty tissue of fish. It moves up the food chain in increased concentration. Once in the bodies of mammals, it's easily measurable and hard to eliminate. It's excreted only through feces, urine and breast milk.

In the spirit of interdisciplinary science, Natalie threw out an idea. "Hey, maybe if we test us humans at the top of the food chain for concentrated mercury, we can extrapolate backwards to profile tuna consumption throughout the world. What do you think?" Dr. Jenkins was lost in thought. "Well, we just tested my wife Dana for mercury, and she might as well be a thermometer. They're already telling her not to breastfeed when she has the baby. Odd that sushi is so expensive and it can concentrate the level of mercury to 600 times the healthy dose.

The three of them leaned on the railing and watched the sunset in silence, until they saw *the green flash,* an optical phenomenon on the horizon caused by the refraction of light by the atmosphere that occurs sometimes as the sun sets over the sea.

This signaled Jenkins that it was time to go home to his wife. He jumped up and rummaged through his pockets for his bike key, and bid them both adieu. "See you in Paris next week, Natalie. Au revoir."

Natalie shared with Spar her thesis dilemma and reluctance to attend the conference as her time was running out. He listened intently. "Natalie, you better not mess around with this. I'd hate to see you back in Dr. Hendershot's thermodynamics class next fall. Once was enough."

She laughed wholeheartedly for the first time in months. "Ya, remember the final when he just stood there and asked, "What is temperature?"

Remembering it well, Spar repeated, "What IS temperature?" Natalie replied, "No, really what IS temperature?" Spar came back with, "No, seriously. What IS temperature?" Maybe it was the beer, maybe it was release of tension after a grueling day, but they just couldn't stop laughing it was so hilarious.

"$t(x) = ax + b$, where t is the temperature of the substance which changes as property x of the substance changes. The constants a and b depend on the substance used and can be evaluated by specifying two temperature points such as 32° for the freezing point of water and 212° for its boiling point, " said a voice.

They both turned around. There was Jamie the Coast Guard guy from the Friends of the River potluck. "You look much happier than the last time I saw you," he said to Natalie. "You fled like Cinderella down those steps. I half expected to see a glass slipper left behind."

Natalie and Spar just stared at him. "Well I could use a fairy godmother about now," she said, still in a stupor from the laughing episode, punctuated by his unexpected appearance.

Jamie extended his hand to Spar. "Hello, I'm Jamie Robertson. U.S. Coast Guard."

On a roll, Spar struggled to keep it funny. "Well EXCU-U-U-SE me!"

"You missed a good meeting," Jamie said to Natalie.

She was perplexed. "What are you doing here?

"Refresher courses," he said. "I'm upgrading my captain's license. I got transferred from Los Angeles to the San Diego Harbor a month ago. How about you?"

"No, I mean what are you doing right here?" she repeated.

"Attending a night class at the Center. I heard the laughing and came to check this place out. You were the last one I expected to see. Especially laughing. Am I interrupting something? Again?"

Spar had disappeared by now and they were alone. "I'm in my last semester of grad school with any luck. And please don't say *refresher courses*," Natalie told him.

The banter continued, "You don't like refresher courses? Why?"

"The shrink. I forgot. Well, Dr. Freud, if I don't submit my PhD thesis by the end of April, I'll be stuck here for another semester or two. Broke and taking refresher courses."

Rebecca, a lab-mate from the food chain group studying plankton, approached them. She looked at the two of them who were acting awkward. She tried to break the ice. "Hello, girl, how's it going? Uh, isn't this happy hour? It's called that for a reason."

Jamie ignored the intruder and focused on Natalie. "May I sit down?" He took a seat on the railing. His silhouette against the post-sunset horizon was impressive. This didn't go unnoticed by Rebecca.

"You may sit anywhere you like," said Natalie with a tone of polite defiance, which was out of character for her. The situation was unsettling. Add a beer, mix in a dose of Chad, and she was a Molotov cocktail.

"Whoa," said Rebecca, wandering off. This wasn't the lab mate she knew. It was the other side of mild-mannered Natalie that she had never seen.

CHAPTER TWELVE
Fishing Village off Alaska
February 18, 8 am

In a small fishing village in the Bering Strait, a huge tuna ship, too big to enter the harbor, was anchored offshore. The crew had come to town in small zodiac boats looking for a home-cooked meal. Native cuisine. They were speaking Russian and the town people were speaking Inuit. The children had gathered around the foreigners out of curiosity.

An old Inuit man turned to his 10-year old grandson. “Don’t tell these people where to catch the best fish, Yutu. They’ve got planes. They don’t need our help.”

In their ancestral tongue, Yutu replied, “We don’t need planes, right pa pa? We know where the fish are. Our ancestors know more than an airplane ever will, right? We only fish for what we need so there will be plenty for our grandchildren.” The old man had a very worried look on his face. “Yes, Yutu. Our people have a different wisdom.”

Later that day, the two were walking the beach when they found a strange and unusual mix of large pelagic fish, dead. Some were not native to the area. The elder stooped to look at them. "Look, Yutu. These fish aren't from around here." He looked to the fishing vessel's enormous wings of nets protruding a thousand feet out on either side. Miles of ropes and long lines were coiled on the bow, and a satellite disk searched the sky. The ship was bigger than the mall up in Anchorage."

"Can you feel that?" The old man whispered as he placed his ear to the sand. There was a vibration his eardrums had never felt before. Though the sound was beyond perception of the human ear, the dogs could hear it and barked. And little Yutu could feel the pulse in the sand beneath his feet.

"This is not good," his grandfather said. "Not good at all."

CHAPTER THIRTEEN
Checkpoint on I-5 at Camp Pendleton
February 15, 2 pm

A caravan of trucks left the weigh station on the I-5 San Diego Freeway, northbound near Camp Pendleton. Another mile up the freeway, the trucks were stopped at the inspection point manned by the U.S. Military. A Mexican driver, the caravan leader, got out of the first vehicle.

The officer motioned him to open his truck and show the contents. "What you got for cargo?"

"Pescado," said the main driver. "Pescado."

The soldier passed from truck to truck directing the main driver to open each back gate, from one to the next. The stench of rotting fish was overwhelming. The rosy face of the young soldier in uniform faded a hue as each gate was swung wide. "Mucho pescado," he said in broken Spanish. "Where did you cross the border? De donde?"

"Tecate."

"And did you declare the *pescado* in Tecate? Where did you get these fish?" At this, the leader went back to his truck and withdrew papers from the glove compartment. The drivers in the other trucks remained motionless.

The soldier read the papers produced by the leader. "Ok, you're from Ensenada. Where are you headed?"

"To the open markets Los Angeles, of course. Abierto mercado. To sell our fish."

"And where exactly are you selling this fish? To whom? Why didn't it go by boat through customs at Long Beach?"

The main driver showed him a purchase order written in Japanese, with a pile of customs declarations. "Wait right there," he told the caravan leader, and took the paperwork into the station booth to scan. In ten minutes, he returned and handed the pile of papers all back to the leader.

"Ok, but you got only until midnight to get up there and right back down over the border—we'll be watching you."

Later, at a shipyard in Long Beach, cranes were lifting boxes from a row of trucks and pouring the contents into a row of water tanks where live fish were swimming around, among dead ones. Illegal Mexicans leapt from the trucks and ran like mice. Meanwhile, a procession of ice trucks backed up to the fish tanks. The larger more lively fish were plucked out of the tanks with a net and thrown into an ice truck. The ice trucks raced to a private airport where hollowed out Gulfstream jets were waiting. One after another, the jets full of live writhing fish left the runway. The less lively ones were poured into a cement truck that ground them up.

CHAPTER FOURTEEN
The Pirates Den Restaurant
Shelter Island, San Diego
February 20, 8 pm

Among the docks on Shelter Island in San Diego Harbor, signs advertised for the whale watching and sport fishing charter boats. In the old days, the sport fishermen could sell their catch to the Bumblee plant across the way, which offered canned tuna to take home in exchange for their fresh catch. It was the sport of hooking them and then reeling them in that drew tourists to the hobby of fishing. Once the hunt was over, so was the thrill. Besides, most of the wives back home drew the line at husbands returning home from guy trips with fish to skin and clean that would stink up the freezer. But now, Bumblee, Starkee, SeaChicken and the other tuna processors had moved to Equador, Puerto Rico, Peru, Chile or to floating canneries in no man's land on the high seas. The restaurants on Shelter Island had taken to buying the fresh catch right off the sport fishing boats, making them an excellent place to dine.

Roy, from Debby's wild night in the Gaslamp District, had invited Debby to his favorite spot, *The Pirates Den.* Debby had agreed to it only if she could invite two surprise guests. Jamie Robertson and Natalie Scott. She came up with the scheme for the surprise rendezvous knowing that Natalie would never agree to a blind date. Neither knew that the other was coming. It was Debby's "get her roommate back on her feet" program. She'd gotten Jamie's number outside of the Friends of the River potluck and had called to invite him out to join some friends. It wasn't Roy's idea of a romantic evening but he was happy to have Debby's attention and was looking forward to meeting the girl in the teeny weeny bikini that he'd seen in the photos at their apartment.

Roy and Debby were seated when Natalie arrived. "Here I am, the third wheel!" she announced. Roy leapt from his seat to pull out her chair. At least Debby's new crush had manners. A good sign, Natalie thought as she sat down. Debby made the introductions. "Natalie Scott, this is Roy... uh." Awkward. She didn't even know his last name. "Santorini," he finished for her. "San-to-rini," she continued. "Roy Santorini, this is Natalie Scott."

The menus arrived and the three of them scanned the six pages of photos. Roy took this opportunity to take command of the conversation with something he thought Natalie would find interesting as an oceanographer. "Oh, they've got tuna tartar. Who knows if it's really tuna. They're getting harder and harder to find, the scarcer they get. Then the Fish and Game shortens the season, reduces the quotas, limits the length and fishermen go out looking for jobs. For people like me, who have been fishermen all their lives, these restrictions threaten our livelihood. What are people like us supposed to do? Wait tables?" When would he stop talking, thought Natalie. He just won't stop. It was going to be a long night.

Roy sensed he was going on and on too much. "So how about you? Debby says you're an oceanographer. What do you study?"

Debby was already a little miffed. Why was he kissing up to Natalie so much? She felt invisible. This might be the first and last date. But she was always game for a good time, so decided to have a little fun.

"Tuna," Debby said.

Roy turned to her, and rubbed her thighs under the table. "You'd like the tuna?"

"No, she studies tuna. That's what Natalie studies. Tuna."

Natalie didn't want to talk about her thesis tonight. She just wanted to feel like a happy-go-lucky co-ed, out having a nice dinner with her friend and her friend's fling. Like a normal person. So, she lopped the ball back into his court. "So, you've been a fisherman all your life?"

Roy pointed to a little skiff at the dinghy dock, named *Time Out.* "I used to have a sport fishing boat and now that's all I've got. My brother and I bailed on it and took jobs with the big guys. But even the big multinational foreign-owned operations are hurting now. The bosses are looking for ways to cut costs." He motioned an imaginary knife cutting his neck.

"You mean bosses like those guys?" A voice popped up from behind them. It was Jamie Robertson and he was pointing to an enormous shiny, white 200-foot yacht docked beyond a gate that read *PRIVATE* at the end of the pier. Purple neon lights the length of the ship spelled out its name, *The Other Girl*. The dinner guests followed Jamie's finger to see a dozen or so well-dressed Japanese executives stepping down the plank, surrounded by boat hands who were helping girls in 6-inch heels negotiate the steep incline.

Him again? This guy just materializes from thin air. Natalie shot Debby a darting glance in regard to the presence of Jamie that read, *what's he doing here?*

"Oh," said Debby, "What a nice surprise!" What a dumb thing to say, she thought. It wasn't a surprise. She had staggered his arrival to be precisely 15 minutes after Natalie's. The little Chinese devil had gotten his phone number after all.

Natalie thought. Sneaky. She hadn't gotten around to telling her roommate that they'd already bumped into each other again at TGIF the night before and it did not go well.

"Well, we just keep bumping into each other," Natalie said with the best smile she could muster considering the trap that had been set for her. The trap that she'd stepped right into hook, line and sinker. It was her turn to make introductions. "Roy Santorini, this is Jamie, uh…" He cut in, "Robertson." Natalie continued, "Jamie Robertson, this is Roy Santorini, and I guess you know Debby Kwan." The look she gave Debby could fry a fish.

Debby gestured to the seat between Natalie and herself. "Please have a seat." Well wasn't she the hostess with the mostest, thought Natalie. It got quiet at this point as each dinner guest struggled to grasp the dynamics of the group. A band in the bar was playing Jimmy Buffet tunes. *Wasting away again in Margaritaville.*

Debby wanted to veer the conversation away from fish. But Roy kept talking, still addressing

Natalie's inquiry about being a fisherman all his life. He wanted to impress them with his knowledge of fish,

"My buddies and I had to give up our sport fishing business. The cost of insurance, maintenance, reservations and bookkeeping was dragging us under, and we had to go out further and further to find fish. Back in those days, many of our customers couldn't take the fish they caught back to Iowa or wherever they were from, so Bumble Bee and Star-kiss-my-ass allowed them to trade their tuna in for cans. Something their wives could handle a little better than some big fish stinkin' up the freezer. We got to know the commercial guys this way, and pretty soon they offered us all a job and we sold our boat to a whale watching outfit.

Roy had now finished his second drink and the waitress placed another in front of him, almost automatically. She also delivered a round of Mai Tai's for the table. Roy was obviously a regular at the *Pirates Den*.

"We don't fly under the flag of the red white and blue anymore. Someday it's Chile, other days it's Guatemala, Brazil or Venezuela. Whoever has a quota to sell, or better yet, you find a country that hasn't joined the Federation and refuses to be assigned a quota at all. Then you're beyond the jurisdiction of anybody—which I think is right incidentally. The ocean is the last frontier."

It was unbelievable how he just kept going and going, drink after drink. Suddenly, Natalie became interested in his lengthy monologue. If only she had brought a pen. Jamie felt the same way and kept Roy going by asking questions. Roy was full of stories that he probably shouldn't be telling either of them. Jamie was in law enforcement and had friends in high places. One of the Coast Guard missions was fisheries enforcement.

"Even if you are stuck with a quota," Roy continued, "there's more than one way to skin a cat. You put the expensive fresh fish on the top and push the lower value ones down into the bilge. Before you get to port, you dump the cheaper ones out the bottom through a trap door in a net. You weight the load so they don't float up to the surface in case there's a raid. I was making over $4k a week until I got a hook in my foot. Dry docked! I can't wait to get back out there again after being dry-docked for months." He went on and on about the ports he had been to all around the world. Debby was mesmerized by his worldliness.

Roy turned to Jamie. "So what do you do?" Debby and Natalie were used to men taking over the conversation as if they weren't even there. For some reason, they didn't mind. Joining in dinner conversations with male egos wasn't all it was chalked up to be.

Jamie didn't answer. Instead, he fiddled with the plastic straw in his drink, avoiding the question. I didn't ask for a straw, he thought, recalling a film he had seen where they found them washed up on shore all over the world and in the stomachs of sea birds, which mistook them for reeds.

Debby made a save. "Hey Roy, you haven't asked me what I do."

Roy winked at Jamie, in a male-bonding sort of way. “I don’t care what you do, baby. It’s what you do to me that counts. You know what they say about sailors in port.”

This was too much to take. “Don’t talk to Debby like that,” Natalie said. Debby looked alarmed. Her plan for a nice dinner was turning into a disaster. She tried to make a save. “So, Roy, where will you be sailing off to?”

Roy was getting even more cocky. “Wherever the fish bite, baby.” He leaned over and gave her a love bite on the cheek.

Natalie was feeling her temper rise. Plus, she was feeling the Mai Tai's which were blurring her judgment, and squelching her manners. “Bite? As if you use hooks. We know you set nets the size of Manhattan.”

“Bigger than Manhattan, actually." He said with bravado. "And our longlines are twelve miles long with a hook every few feet."

Natalie couldn't believe how obnoxious he was. "The bycatch are dead by the time you reel them in. I don't think you should be bragging about plundering the ocean."

Roy needed to regain the upper hand. "Anyway, Debby, let's make up for lost time in advance. The boat's going to be at the shipyard getting some retrofits before we leave. Come to my bunkroom and I'll show you my *etchings*. At this point, he began to display his tattoos.

Oddly, Debby was falling for him, whereas some girls might be revolted. His sexual innuendoes turned her on.

Roy turned back to Jamie. "So what do you do?" Jamie all but saluted his reply, "U.S. Coast Guard, sir."

In a way that only a drunk person can get serious, Roy took on a professional air. "Hey, this is all off the record, right? I guess when you're at sea all the time, you get, you know, anti-social. You need to talk to people." Then he switched the topic and turned back to Debby. "Hey, need anything from Alaska? We're heading up to through the Bering Strait next month."

Still oblivious to Roy's distasteful nature, Debby gave him an affectionate shoulder bump. "I hear the ratio up there is 7 to 1 men to women, so I'm not worried."

Roy had a comeback for everything. "On the boat it's about 300 to 0, so I think you're safe there too."

Natalie let the comment go, practicing a meditation technique to divert her temper. She thought of her days at sea when she was single. "With odds up that high, any girl would be a fool to join the crew, especially if she was unattached."

Debby turned to her. "What do you mean? Those are great odds for a girl."

"The odds are you'll be harassed." said Natalie who knew what she was talking about. Single women at sea were inevitably hunted down day and night like wild beasts. "Why do you think I got married to Chad so quickly? I was at sea all the time with an all-man crew. If you don't have a ring on your finger you get mauled." She started looking sad again.

“Let’s dance,” said Jamie. The band was playing *Little Surfer*. It was a slow song. He could finally find a way to comfort this girl with the broken heart. He wanted to make her feel like everything was going to be ok. “We’ll join you,” said Debby speaking for Roy and pulling his hand. They all got up to find the dance floor.

At the end of the song the two girls caught up in the ladies room. They were standing at the mirror touching up hair and make-up when Natalie finally said what was on her mind. “Congratulations,” said Natalie. “You’re dating a first class jerk.”

Debby did a baby doll pout. “C’mon I’m just having a little fun. He’ll be gone in a few days. But your guy, I say he’s a keeper.

“My guy? Debby, you called him? Don’t you think you might have asked me?”

“You wouldn’t have come,” she said, and she was probably right.

Natalie didn’t even bother to bring up the fact that she’d already bumped into him again since the potluck, and that it was a bust. “Well, at least he’s a gentleman.”

Debby poofed up her friend's hair and gave her a hug. “Gentlemen, shmentlemen. He’s dreamy. You gotta give him a chance. This is no dress rehearsal. Chill! Live, honey.” Soon they were having fun and looking fabulous together just the way it used to be. Yin and Yang. “Hey, Natalie, remember in ninth grade when you were too intimidated to go to the prom with that hot tenth grader and you stayed home that night? He’s the tenth grader and this is your second chance." Debby pushed her out the door and they left the ladies room together giggling like teenagers.

CHAPTER FIFTEEN
The ITC Convention, Paris
February 21, 3 pm

Natalie and Salt were manning the NOAA booth at the ITC conference, passing out information pamphlets on ABNJ, ocean areas that lie beyond national jurisdiction and remain ungoverned, thus exploited by the greediest of the human species. "Just smile and look smart," said Salt to Natalie. "Maybe you'll land a husband," he joked. Natalie grinned in a wincing nervous sort of way as though it made her stomach hurt to smile. Ouch!

It was a good time for Salt and Natalie to look for clues on where the bluefin were hiding and to share notes. She asked him what he thought about the North American Free Trade Agreement. Whether Canada and Mexico's fishing restrictions were lifted. How to include protection of the high seas in the UN Convention on the Law of the Sea when their own country, and Venezuela and Russia refused to sign on. It was like the wild, wild west out there now, he told her. All the while, the free for all was driving down the fish prices and putting U.S. fleets out of business. The Mexican boats kept trespassing the 200-mile limit, getting closer and closer to the marine protected areas that environmentalists had been fighting so hard for. In many cases, marine sanctuaries were just a fancy name. No-take zones couldn't be enforced because they couldn't be monitored and trespassers knew it. American companies were flying Chilean flags on their vessels to avoid quotas and who knows what. Brazil was buying up marine survey technology like there was no tomorrow. It was impossible to fully understand what was going on beyond what Fish and Wildlife called 'see level.' Satellites were on the brink of deciphering shipping vessels from fishing vessels by patterns received from their AIS signals. That's if the signals weren't intentionally disabled. But who was going to pay for crunching all that data? As they talked, Salt noticed the book *Ocean Bankruptcy by Stephen Sloan* poking out of Natalie's purse.

"A little light reading?" he asked, and began flipping through it. He noticed some of his own publications listed in the bibliography in the back.

Next to the NOAA booth was a group called *Carbon Offset*. The monitor was playing clips from *An Inconvenient Truth* and other climate change films, attracting a crowd. Either that, or the people were simply making a play for the candy dish. The person handling the booth explained, "The problem is people think carbon offsets are some kind of new weight loss fitness program. When really, carbon emissions are destroying our oceans. The atmosphere interacts constantly with the ocean surface, which is over 70% of the Earth's surface. Emissions from fuel combustion are saturating the water column making our oceans more acidic. This is dissolving the protective shells of corals and destroying healthy coral reefs, the buffer zone that shelters our coastlines. Lobsters, crabs, and the skeletal structures of fish and mammals throughout the food chain are all at risk… Here, take a brochure…"

The NOAA booth wasn't as popular. "We need a candy dish," said Natalie.

Just then there was a customer. He was a slight sepia-toned man with bluish lips. The semicircles beneath his eyes had the look of coffee cup stains. To the credit of his appearance he was dressed in a starched blue-collared short sleeve shirt that made his water-blue eyes pop. As he closed in on the booth he gave off a complex bouquet of curry, deodorant and spiced aftershave, just a note or two away from homeopathic bug spray. This did not deter a chubby and persistent fly from buzzing relentlessly around his head. The man was passing out brochures. "Hello, I am Srinivas from *Count It*. We do marine surveys for various governments, to fit in any budget. We know how tight the research funds are these days. Let us give you an estimate." His name tag read, *No job too small… or too big.*

Natalie recognized the company name *Count It* from her database.

Just then, a pretty activist from Greenpeace stopped at the booth and began to question Srinivas in a voice that was laced with interrogation. “So, how does your company *Count It's* compensation work? I’ve heard you pay your people by the number of surveys they turn in, not by salary. If you pay only by number of fish counted, this encourages, or should I say incentivizes, your workers to trump up data? On Martha’s Vineyard, didn't they catch one of the supervisors fudging surveys and coaching summer college workers to do the same? Do you think this data you supply to governments is accurate enough to be used as a basis for the population projections that determine quotas?” She asked one more question, looking him straight in the eye, and leaning in. “Did you know that the accuracy of this data determines the sustainable future of the ocean?” Srinivas looked overly indignant by this, shifting from one foot to another until she finished her inquisition. He had an answer all ready for her. This was nothing new. His boss had been all over the news for the discrepancies she was referring to. They’d hired a PR company to handle it, which had armed the sales staff with talking points in preparation for such rude accusations.

“Thank you for asking, Ms…?” he said, grinning at the small group which had formed.

“Michelle Donahue from Greenpeace," she replied, implying aggression with her tone and leaning in further.

Thank you for asking Mrs. Donahue. Or, excuse me Miss!" he sympathized focusing directly on her unadorned wedding finger. This well-rehearsed intimidation move succeeded as it did with most single women, as evidenced by the pink flush that spread up her neck, flooding her face. "It gives me an opportunity to clear up the misunderstanding caused by the negative press. *Count It* pays $6/hour for a 2-hour assignement. It’s a career opportunity to help needy students break into marine science. They pay for their own transportation and training to prove their commitment, and they must read the operation manual, become familiar with the nautical charts, and memorize the fish identification guide on their own time. Again to prove their commitment. I can’t tell you how competitive these jobs are. We select the best and the brightest as part of our mission to train young scientists. It's a STEM initiative..." Here, waving away the fly, he addressed the cluster of onlookers again who were drawn to the scene like amused spectators at a gladiator fight. "That's the nation's campaign for higher education in Science, Technology, Engineering and Math which is at the core of our mission. We pay an additional $6 for each interview they have with fishermen who are actively fishing, which they fax to us within 4 hours or we don't pay. It keeps them honest. Naturally, the more data they collect, the more they get paid."

The *Count It* sales rep then turned his back to Michelle, the Greenpeace worker, chuckled, and faced Natalie and Salt who held perfectly still, dumbfounded. Salt had served as an expert witness in the ongoing trial against *Count It*, who had done an excellent job of covering their tracks and dodging subpoenas thanks to an army of defense lawyers who also worked for the mob. Srinivas was oblivious. "Here is my card. I see you are with NOAA. We have worked together for years. We have a long-standing relationship on the Large Pelagic Fish Survey. We only charge you $97 per survey, a 50% discount because we think what you are doing is so important." As was his nature, Salt showed no expression, revealing nothing on either his face or in his body language, a posture he had perfected in the military.

"Oh boy," said Michelle, rolling her eyes toward the guy. "Now I've heard everything," she said looking at Natalie. "These people faked fish counts to make more money and pinch the government. Taxpayers were paying for *Count It* to provide fake fish data is what it came down to. Then the public pays for it again in the decline of fish populations because of them. I hope your boss is indicted for a white collar crime. The problem is, that won't bring the fish population back that you've decimated with your phony, trumped up data."

Srinivas laughed at such a preposterous idea. Unfettered, Michelle continued. "The press said they weren't students, but retired fisheries employees augmenting their pensions. When you pay by the survey, you provide incentive to make them up. And because the governments pay you by the survey, the cards are stacked in your favor to fabricate numbers. It was a whale watching boat that turned you in, right? Didn't you report their boat license number as a sport fishing boat? I read that you created fake catches and surveys and paid workers an extra at $6 a pop. The supervisors hired starving college kids who were untrained and unmonitored. They just faxed in the bogus surveys and got a check in the mail. Nice way to train young scientists! Then you went off and sold the surveys to the government. In turn, they used these exaggerated numbers to model the fish population and come up with the very quotas that would maintain the health of the fisheries. Then you sold the data again to the fishing industry. They aren't your fish. You are playing with the very future of our planet. Basically you sell bogus data to the government that is used to sustain fish populations for future generations. How much do you make at *Count It*, Srinivas? The article said your CEO has houses all over the world, his own island, his own plane, and a superyacht." Then she lowered her voice and got right up in ear, "And some say he owns majority stock in a fleet of cannery boats.

Srinivas remained unflinching. “We have something called overhead, Miss Donahue. Administration, sales and marketing. How do you think we can afford to sponsor these conferences?" he said pointing to the enormous banner bearing the name of *Count It* that stretched across the ceiling. The conference sponsorship also earned them a speaker position on the panel titled, *The Future of Fish*. "We can’t have a supervisor on every ship, on every boat launch, and in every port. The discrepancy discovered by the press was a lie that was completely fabricated by a disgruntled employee. No evidence was found to verify his report. Our data is the best in the biz. I’ll vouch for that. And we pass the savings on to good people like… them,” he said, directing his full attention back to Salt and Natalie.

Salt knew the whole story. The surveys had suddenly disappeared when Congress demanded to see them. Nobody knew just how many extra fish had been reported. He flashed his signature tight-lipped schoolboy smile at Srinivas. “Scientists like Natalie here actually use that data to help save our oceans.”

Natalie stared down at Srinivas' alligator shoes and felt wheels turning in her brain. She'd been using the data, for one thing. And the government was listed as a client right on *Count It's* brochure.

The Feds were still buying data from these guys because of a bulletproof, long-term contract. What a wicked world. She suddenly needed a margarita. Do they have them in France?

CHAPTER SIXTEEN
Mr. and Mrs. Scotts' house
Martha's Vineyard
February 19, 3 pm

Mr. Scott reached for the headphone set that his younger daughter, called Nat the Nerd by her sister, had given him for Christmas. He put it on his head.

From the kitchen his wife of 25 years was watching him. "What are you doing Herman?" she called in her friendly Midwestern twang. Margaret knew that Herman and their daughter Natalie talked a lot on the phone. Sometimes she even felt a little left out. Even jealous. At worse times, she imagined that the whole world was out to get her. But her voice never showed it. She was of the 1920's when I was inappropriate to do much but get along with people.

"I'm connecting with *marrrrtians*, Margaret," he called to his wife, teasing her.

She looked at him and crinkled up her nose playfully. His doctor said he had early signs of Alzheimer's but that wasn't a problem for her. She'd gotten the same diagnosis. They were aging in parallel. His travels in and out of reality amused her most of the time. He just went off into his own little world. And truthfully, that had always been the part of him that she loved the most. He was a dreamer.

"Don't worry, Margaret, I won't tell them where we live!" he called again. He blew her a kiss. She continued to water the violets on the windowsill.

Out the window she could see that the dirt road to town was pooled with water. She surmised that it had been an unusual high tide the night before. She thought she'd wait for them to dry up before taking the Subaru to town for groceries.

The two of them together were happy on Martha's Vineyard for the most part, living out their old age on an outcrop of glacial moraine in the Atlantic Ocean. The island was a potpourri of breathtaking farms and ranches, quaint coastal coves, fresh ponds, botanical gardens, hiking trails, mature forests, and lovely stretches of sandy beaches. It was also lush with history, from the early tribes that occupied the land for thousands of years, to the onslaught of the whaling industry centuries ago that had made Martha's Vineyard and Nantucket famous around the world.

Herman had spent his childhood summers there on the island with his grandparents and it held a special place in his heart. Later, his father had moved into the house and built the garage after retirement. After he passed on, Herman convinced Margaret that Martha's Vineyard was the place to retire.

They fell into a seasonal routine using the winter to read, sew needlepoints, carve woodworks, and explore new hobbies. In spring they planted the garden. In summer their daughters came, one with their two grandchildren who loved the beach and the thrill of the throngs of kids riding their bikes all over the island.

In August, Herman and Margaret entered their handicrafts in the Agricultural Fair. The population shrank from 100,000 to 20,000 when summer was over. Fall was the time of glorious weather and warm water thanks to the Gulfstream Current that brought it up from the topics. There was the perfect number of year-round and shoulder-season people, and it became a tight and caring community with a surprising number of activities.

They could join clubs, including boards that decided who could build what, where and how, and what land should be left in its natural state. Who got a commercial liquor license and who didn't. Public access to beaches. Low income housing. Paper vs plastic. These board meetings were televised by the local access station and were free to anyone who bought cable service. They could get just dramatic enough to capture the viewer's attention and Herman was one of them.

The island had plenty of things to do for the Scotts, who enjoyed the small town lifestyle. On any given day, somewhere on the island there was something to do. There were square dances, fishing derbies, film festivals, off-season yacht club socials in Edgartown, day trips to lectures in Woods Hole and handicraft circles. Consistent throughout the year were the melodies of waves that kept time, the remarkable sunrises and sunsets against a current of clouds above, the ferry's foghorn and the call of gulls that sang them to sleep each night and woke them each morning.

Herman was fumbling with the headphones and the voice device. He plugged the whole contraption into the phone and settled back into his favorite chair by the picture window with the horizon of the sea straight ahead.

“Natalie? May I please speak with Natalie? It’s her old man,” he chuckled. “Can you hear me? Oh, she’s in Paris?” He cuffed the phone and reported this to his wife. “She’s in Paris, mother.” That was what he called his wife in the presence of their girls.

Calls from Mr. Scott were nothing new to Lily the receptionist in Natalie's lab. Mr. Scott liked to keep tabs on his daughter and she thought it was touching. She often went out of her way to assure Mr. Scott that Natalie was ok, even if she had no idea where she was. She didn't want him to worry. He was a good-natured gentleman who insisted that she call him Herman. She was touched by how much he cared. Her own dad didn't even know where she worked.

"Natalie is with the National Oceanic and Atmosphere Administration at ITC. Yes, at a conference in Paris. Yes, NOAA. Yes, the International Tuna Convention."

Herman started to imagine he was talking to his daughter. "NOAA. Yes, why didn't you just say that, dear? Oh, at the ITC? Keep your passport with you, and a money belt."

"It's just me, Mr. Scott. Lily at reception."

"Ok, honey, I just wanted to know that you're ok." He cuffed his hand over the speaker and spoke in a whisper so his wife could not overhear him. “So… tell me… did you find the fish yet?”

Lily was lost for words and claimed to have a bad connection, rapping the phone with a pencil eraser.

Margaret put down her watering can. “What on Earth are you talking about? What fish? Check the freezer!"

CHAPTER SEVENTEEN
Tuna Convention
February 19, 11 am

Natalie was perusing the rows of rows of booths at convention when she was hailed by a man at a booth waving madly at her with one of his hands. In the other, he was clenching a phone and yelling at it in Portuguese. The logo on his booth identified his company as *Ocean Enterprises* with its motto, *On Top of the Food Chain*.

Natalie looked at this crazy man who was wildly motioning to her. Not recognizing him, she checked around the floor to see if maybe she had dropped something. He pointed right at her, and then at himself. When he was off the phone, he used the other hand to pound at his heart like a gorilla. Salvador Domingo had been attending ITC for years, and had never seen a sight like Natalie. In a desert of men in overstuffed suits and bearded guys in safari attire, she was like a mirage. In a bold dramatic gesture, he got down on one knee in the middle of the aisle and took her hand.

“Come, please. Talk to me. Where are you from?” Slightly amused by this act of chauvinism, she answered. “I’m from California.” She laughed for the first time all day.

“I will show you the world. Come with me. We will go straight to my private jet the second they roll up the carpets and tear down the kiosks. Oh, I see you don’t believe me?” he said with puppy dog eyes. “But, look!” he exclaimed and pulled a photo out of his suit pocket with the grand style of a great magician. “Here is my jet.” Sure enough, there was a picture of Salvador Domingo standing in the door of a Gulfstream P-17. “Where do you want to go? Any place you desire. Come, sit. My heart is leaping like a flying fish. Save me!” he said hooking his mouth with his finger and flapping around in the aisle like a fish being caught. He pulled her to a chair at the *Ocean Enterprises* booth and offered her the candy dish. He flashed the biggest, whitest collection of teeth she had ever seen.

“Who are you here with? Tell me he’s not more handsome than I am. She answered, “I’m working with NOAA here at the conference." she Salvador Domingo slipped Natalie his calling card. "Why are you with them when you could be working for me? I'll give you a job right now and you'll have more riches that you've ever dreamed of. Including my crown jewels. He grabbed her hand to his crotch before she could yank it back. "Plus with this job comes a big bonus."

He called after her, "Hey pretty science lady - if you can get a million dollars for a live, writhing tuna in Tokyo, it beats selling dead fish for fertilizer. Let's face it."

Staggering away in shock, Natalie scanned the exhibit hall for an EXIT sign and escaped from the humiliation out the back entrance. Her brain felt like it was sloshing around in her head. And it was only day two!

An hour later, Natalie was still reeling from the humiliation by the *Ocean Enterprises* jerk when she returned to the exhibit hall. On her way back to her post at NOAA, she stopped at the French Surfriders table to get her mind off of him. She picked up a DVD entitled *Poisson Poison*, next to the mailing list sign-up sheet. Manning this booth was the same surfer girl who also was pictured on the cover of the DVD and on the film poster hanging from the table. "Pourquoi?" she asked Natalie pointing to her nametag. Natalie looked puzzled. "Part of your nom," the girl asked. "Why, excuse my bad English, uh, barree docteur? Why did you cross out docteur?" Natalie realized she was referring to her name badge credentials, hanging around her neck on a lanyard. "Oh, I haven't finished yet. My PhD I mean. They made a mistake at registration."

The girl shook her head, and put out her hand. Je m'appelle Jeanette Dubois. "I don't speak English so good. Juste un petit peu. Attendant s'il vous plait… A moment please." The other woman in the booth spoke English and was the producer of *Poisson Poison.* This was a warm and kind relief from Natalie's last trade show booth encounter. "You are from NOAA?" the woman asked.

That was another nametag confusion. “No, I’m actually just a student at the Ocean Center in La Jolla, California. What’s your film about?”

The producer handed her another DVD. Here, you can have two. Let us know what you think.” Surfriders are the most powerful advocates for ocean conservation here in France. Would you like to be on the mailing list?” Natalie knew the organization well. “I belong to the San Diego Chapter.” She liked the Surfriders. Many of them were also Friends of the River. “Could you put it on this?” Natalie said handing them her NOAA thumbdrive.

While they loaded the video, Natalie studied the fish on the poster. Wahoo, Mahi Mahi, Big Eye Tuna, Bluefin Tuna, Mako, Marlin, Swordfish, Yellowtail, and Sharks all swimming along what appeared to be an extinction graph, highlighting the species that were disappearing the most rapidly. Without these predators, the sea would be a broth of soup consisting of the bottom of the food chain. When these top predators were gone, the jellyfish would have a field day.

Natalie visited booth after booth, collecting information and making new friends. There were undersea exploration companies, underwater webcam manufacturers, seismic sonar engineers, NGOs, military career recruiters, photographers, virtual reality experiential programs, and diving games. Roaming the aisles, she bumped into the taggers from Stanford. The bright, eager faces of the undergrads reminded her of herself back then. The young taggers were doing a lot to shed light on the truth about threats to the ocean food chain that, once toppled, would not right itself. Not in Natalie's lifetime. Their combined data of 23 species showed two hotspots where migration routes concentrated in the north Pacific. Undergrads named them after the two fast food giants, McDonald's and Burger King. One ran east to west between Hawaii and Alaska along a temperature transition boundary between cold sub-Arctic waters and warmer subtropical waters. The other was the California Current, which ran south along the west coast of California. Historically, these were the locations where food was most abundant and easy to come by. The productivity at the bottom of the food chain in this area was often compared to the great savannah grasslands of Africa, where the world's greatest land predators came to dine. Thus, it got its nickname, the Blue Serengeti.

CHAPTER EIGHTEEN
The Hotel de Paris
February 20, 4 pm

Finally, back at the hotel resting from jet lag and sensory overstimulation, Natalie lay on her bed flat on her stomach. She was reading the PR kit for French Surfriders film, *Poisson Poison*. She popped in the thumb drive that was given to her by the Surfriders, and loaded the movie on her laptop.

In the film, the surfer girl from the booth, Jeanette Dubois, was the reporter who was speaking on camera. She was interviewing Jeremy Hart, Director of Greenpeace, on the Rainbow Warrior vessel. He spoke English with French subtitles. He was talking about tuna fleet flag switching. "Let's say your fishing fleet is flying a Chinese flag giving you a quota of 10 tons a week. You're on your way to port with your ten tons and you find a school of 500-pound bluefin and catch five more tons. What are you going to keep? The fish that will fetch you a million dollars apiece, or the ones you can sell for fishmeal and fertilizer that are stinking up the bilge?"

Then a mock advertisement spot came up for a pretend product called *I Can't Believe It's Not Fish.* A man in a grocery aisle held up a box of the product from the frozen food section. The commercial showed the man pouring fish parts into a blender. Bones, eyeballs, scales, fins, guts, teeth and all. As gruesome as it was, Natalie laughed out loud. Funny. Humor had a way of being more effective than doom and gloom. It was true. Most of the bigger boats had the grinders on board these days they blended everything up and froze it into some kind of disgusting fish gumbo for cat food, fertilizer and fishmeal, right on the spot. Other products were molded and printed from the substance, to look like shrimp, crab and lobster.

The film cut back to Jeannette after the commercial and she looked at the camera, all bummed out. "But who is regulating this behavior?" The film cut to Greenpeace director Jeremy Hart, holding up a report that was their plan to save the oceans, *Roadmap to Recovery, a Global Network of Marine Reserves.* He talked about Areas Beyond National Jurisdiction known at the UN as ABNJ. It's a no man's land that includes most of the ocean, where unbridled, mega-conglomerate, multinational corporations are running the show. Undercover shadow companies played musical chairs with country flags and have false bottom boats, fish finders, drones, fish grinders, private jets, helicopters, satellites, submarines, artificial reefs, fish magnets, and highly sophisticated detection technology. "You name it, they got it," he said. "They can afford it! They are raping the world's ocean for all it's worth. This is our children's common , not theirs. How do we stop them?" It was true. The technology these boats have was more sophisticated than the NASA space program, all for personal gain. This was not about feeding the masses. "We need to declare marine protected areas," he proclaimed. "The ones who are fighting against the protected areas are those who want to hoard our planet's resources that don't belong to them. At the rest of the world's expense. Protected areas help tourism and local fishers who are nearly extinct too."

Natalie knew they were right. The deep sea is out of sight, out of mind for every day citizens.

The public had no idea what was going on. Ignorance is dangerous. It sets the perfect scenario for foul play. Jeanette Dubois had a way of stating the facts while engaging the crowd. The ivory tower of the science world needed messengers like Jeanette to send out SOS signals. That's exactly what scientists are trained not to do. Science is the deepest dive in the pursuit of knowledge. Those who loved the mental gymnastics of pure science were the lucky ones, Natalie thought. But it required the relentless discipline of investigation and persistent inquiry. Most people have a limited attention span for science. Natalie was feeling better knowing that people like Jeanette were paying attention to research results and towing the line. It was refreshing.

Until now, Natalie's understanding of the commercial fishing industry was only peripheral. The underworld. In the short time that she'd been working on her thesis, this out-of-control, uneconomic, ungoverned, corporate-owned, government-backed industry had hooked, netted, exploded, filtered and poisoned the seas to death. The same thing was happening in the mining industry.

Was the world being run by madmen? The sane people were figuring out how to pick up the pieces. Or was it the other way around? Were humans meant to be conscious? If so, why was this happening? So there were the destroyers creating the problems and others trying to solve the problems. The destructive practices made some people rich, and the rest of the world poor. Research institutions kept raising money to study how to fix everything. It was an uphill climb when it came to public support for pure science. Most people will never see the ocean except for a logo on the side of a can romanticizing fish as the chicken of the sea.

Natalie turned off the film, her head too full. She gazed out the beveled, leaded window. The streets of Paris were full of couples strolling the busy lanes together thinking of little but love, or so she imagined. She was only twenty-seven. Way too young to be bitter.

CHAPTER NINETEEN
An international commercial jet
February 21, 4 pm

Natalie's flight back home to southern California crossed the Atlantic Ocean, the North American continent, dipped over downtown San Diego, crossed Interstate 5, and touched down on the runway of the Lindberg Field. Her sister Sally had driven down from Oceanside to pick her up at the airport and had arrived too early. Sally was circling the arrival terminals on the lower level, pausing just long enough to be waved away by traffic cops as the curb announcement repeated itself, "The white zone is for loading and unloading only. No parking." Impatient, when she finally saw her sister Natalie emerge from baggage claim, Sally leaned heavily on the horn, and popped the trunk. Soon they were on their way over Point Loma to Natalie's apartment in Ocean Beach.

"Dad says he talked to you in Paris?" Sally asked in a tone that only meant one thing. A disagreement. For two girls who shared the same basic DNA, sometimes they felt as different as night and day. Sally was intent on correcting their dad when he became delusional. She felt it was important to set the record straight and keep his mind on track. Natalie didn't think it mattered and saw no point in telling Sally that she had not spoken to him in Paris.

They drove quietly over Point Loma to Ocean Beach just as the sun was setting turning the sky to an orange, lemon and lime sherbet. The string of lights across the Coronado Bridge came on behind them and looked a string of diamonds against the rainbow sky. Natalie was glad to be home.

Finally, she responded to Sally. "No, I did not talk with dada in Paris, Sal. He was probably talking to my phone receptionist named Lily and didn't know the difference. And yes, he still thinks I'm still married to Chad, too. It doesn't matter."

Sally remained as adamant as a lion tamer about keeping Mr. Scott's mind on point. "Why don't you just tell him about Chad again?"

"What's the point? He's old. Just let him think whatever makes him feel happy. Marriage is happy. Divorce is not happy. By the way, how's yours? How's your marriage?" she said changing the topic.

Sally was fighting back tears. "I'm pregnant again and Billy doesn't want me to work at the travel agency anymore."

The world's most pressing problems didn't exist for Sally, Natalie thought. She had a marvelous ability to focus only on her immediate surroundings. At the slightest imperfection in her appearance or that of her home, she became unglued. This also applied to everything and everyone around her. Conquering chaos with order gave her life meaning. She was coiffed and well dressed. They were opposites but growing up alongside of each other taught them tolerance and mutual respect. They loved one another but not with adoration. It was a dutiful love bonded by their parents, their past, and their shared genetics. If called upon they would risk their lives for each other, but on a day to day basis it was more of a tug of war.

If someone told Natalie to just stay home and have children right now, she'd jump over the moon. "So, Sally, just stay home, watch the kids and decorate. Maybe he'll get bored of you and send you back to work. Take up a new hobby. Tiling. I saw some hand-painted tiles in Paris that were truly marvelous. You could enter them in the Ag Fair on the Vineyard over the summer."

"While you're flying off to Paris to fancy meetings, and getting your PhD?" Sally exclaimed. Natalie was afraid this conversation would take them to a new low. It was unfathomable that Sally was actually envious of her little sister. She had the successful husband, smart kids, two dogs and an actual white picket fence. Oh, and a nanny. Natalie cut her sister a lot of slack, though. When Finn died, Sally was the glue who held the family together when everyone was falling apart. She was especially good in crisis. But it took a crisis to bring out that side of her. In between it was mostly melodrama.

"Look, it's not as glamorous as it seems, Sally. You don't even want to know. So, are you going to call ma and dad and tell them you're having another baby? Or do I have to? They'll be happy, seeing as I'm not perpetuating their genes. Go forth and procreate! By the way, I hope you aren't eating fish."

Sally really detested talking about the environment, or other political issues as she called them. She found it unbecoming on her sister, too. "I thought fish was brain food. Now we can't eat it anymore? That sounds like a joke, Natalie."

Natalie made one last ditch effort before dropping it. Not as much for her sister, but for her niece or nephew-to-be. There was scientific evidence that mercury in fish was the lead paint epidemic of the times. But though buildings and windowsills could be scraped and stripped of lead, mercury could not be removed from the ocean. Coal-burning power plants were spewing mercury into the atmosphere and out over the ocean at an alarming rate. Like other emissions, mercury got absorbed by the sea. It sank into the world where the fish lived and filtered seawater through their gills for oxygen. Then it worked its way through the food chain. Already the education system was preparing for an onslaught of children with impaired learning abilities. Natalie couldn't imagine her sister raising a special needs child.

"No, I'm not kidding. The mercury gets absorbed into the blood, into the placenta and even into your hair. I'll prove it to you." Having arrived at her apartment, she leaned over to give her sister a kiss on the cheek, and plucked a hair from her head to give to Spar. "I love you. Thanks for picking me up. Say hi to Billy and the kids."

"Ow!" Sally rubbed her hair follicle and watched her sister in rear view mirror as she unloaded her luggage. Natalie had always been obsessed by the sea. It was probably from spending all that time walking the beach in the mornings with dad. Natalie was their dad's favorite and that sometimes stung like a jellyfish.

CHAPTER TWENTY
San Diego Harbor entrance jetty
February 22, 8 pm

Six of the Bottom Scratchers were crowded into a Boston Whaler, all suited up with tanks for the night dive, on a mission to help Fish and Game confiscate illegal lobster traps along the San Diego Harbor entrance jetty. It was a dark night with no moon. The tanks clanged gently as they motored out along Point Loma against with the last stretch of an outgoing tide that was just about reverse. They anchored the boat just inside the swells in the protection of the south jetty. The plan was to find the unlicensed, illegal lobster traps, float them up, and free the catch. The game wardens would then dispose of the traps properly.

The dive was timed precisely to catch a lull between the ebb and flow of the swift current that funneled the massive volume of water in and out of the bay twice a day. Into the pockets of their buoyancy compensators, the divers tucked their knives, flashlights, line, and lift bags they would fill with air to float the traps to the surface.

As the tide reversed in the harbor channel, the currents became complex and varied by depth. Also, there were sporadic eddies that spun like a flushing toilet. The divers had agreed to tether themselves to a buddy so that nobody would drift off. Al Stover from the dive locker was Natalie's buddy. He signaled to her, and backflipped off the bow. She tossed him her tether line, and jumped in behind him. Everyone else followed.

Their flashlights flipped on and together they descended down the anchor line. The angle of the rope line indicated that the tide was indeed flowing in. Better than out, thought Natalie as she caught up with Al who was waiting on the bottom blowing air bubbles in the shape of smoke rings like he was enjoying a cigarette. She laughed but laughing is tricky with a regulator in your mouth. They gave on another the a-okay sign and worked their way down the base of the jetty looking for traps, trying not to kick up sand to further limit the visibility.

The Bottom Scratchers found illegal traps right away. Lots of them. Each one had its own distinctly colored buoy with the number etched out. They floated cleverly floated just below the sea surface to be imperceptible to the Fish and Game wardens. They swam from trap to trap, clipping the lines off with carabineers.

Out the corner of her mask, Natalie noticed a pale blur. Not sure if it was a seal or a dolphin or something else, she checked her tether line to Al. She'd had enough experience with both dolphins and seals to know that they were playful as puppies and equally a nuisance. They'd play with your line, your fins, and put their cute little faces right up to your mask if you let them. All fun and games until someone or something got tangled. Soon, Natalie got nudged. A dolphin, bumped her with its snout so she'd tickle its brow. To dolphins, everything seemed like a joke. They had the night vision of an infrared camera so there was no hiding from these characters. This one was yucking it up like a prankster right in her face. She gave it a pet on the head and then nudged it away. She tossed a rock for it to go chase like a dog, just to get its adorable little squeaking snout out of her way. Just then she noticed Al getting bumped by another one while he was inflating a lift bag with air from his regulator to float a trap. His regulator dropped from his mouth and he was kicking like crazy not to get pushed into the fast current of the harbor's inner channel. But the dolphins thought he was playing a game and kept bumping him for fun. Natalie grabbed Al's fin and stuck his regulator in his mouth. It must be hard for a dolphin to understand that people can't hold their breath. Once Al got himself together, he reached into his BC and pulled out some crime scene tape that dolphins and seals liked to play with. He trailed it behind him, swinging it like a jump rope for the dolphins to play with. Leave it to Al to come well prepared. Even through the mask you could see that childish glint in his 80-year old eyes. He'd spent as much of his life underwater as topside. For all Natalie knew, the dolphins recognized him and were just trying to get his goat.

She and Al rested for a moment at the next trap. They had kicked up a lot of sand and the visibility was worse. The two buddies did an equipment check for each other, and began to inch their way up current back toward the boat. It didn't take long to encounter another trap.

Al clipped off the buoy and prepared the lift bag again to help float the trap. In the old days they floated the traps up to the surface by inflating their buoyancy compensator vests, a practice that went out of style when a diver dropped a trap in sixty feet of water and shot up to the surface like a cork. Losing two atmospheres of pressure on his body so fast caused the compressed gasses in his blood stream to expand and burst his arteries. From the surface of the ocean to the heavens, humans live under one atmosphere of pressure. Once descended to 30 feet, add another one from the dense pressure of the sea. Another 30 feet, and that's two atmospheres. Fill your lungs down there with canned air, and shoot to the surface without exhaling and the air expands in your membranes and basically your lungs can burst.

These makeshift lift bags were safer and lightened the load from pulling them up by hand. They were designed by Al, ever the inventor. He had a motto. Dive with your brain, not your back.

Natalie peered inside the next trap with her flashlight. One 10-pound molting adult, and three ¼-pound juveniles. She unhitched the trap door and grabbed a little juvenile, and sent it off scurrying to safety among the boulders of the jetty. When there was time, she loved setting them free on the bottom vs. throwing them overboard from the boat. Poor things.

Al watched her through her air bubbles and thought about how much Natalie truly cared about the residents of the sea. She was a kind and caring person. Like his own wife. Even *he* was upset with Chad. He had given the swine his first job, filling tanks for him in the dive locker. The guy was an idiot.

Eventually the two divers gave each other a thumb's up and they ascended together to the surface to look for the boat. If it was a distance away, they'd go back down and swim on the bottom by the jetty where the water was calm. They were relieved to see the boat close by.

They fully inflated their buoyancy compensators to float and savor the evening's starry skies.

"Did you see that 10-pounder? Pretty big for a spiny," said Natalie. "Thanks for distracting that dolphin," he said gazing up at the heavens. He just loved this stuff. They signaled the boat with flashlights to come pick them up. The others were relieved to see them bobbing on the surface. They'd been gone awhile. "Gentlemen, start your engines," announced the diver at the wheel. "And don't run us over!" Al called back. The Boston Whaler pulled up next to them and soon they were back on the boat.

It was piled high with the confiscated wire-style, west coast variety, lobster traps. The divers set about letting lobsters go, and stacked the traps to hand them over to the authorities. There was a 10-pound lobster that was tempting to keep. And eat, or sell. Al Stover held up his hand. "We are not poachers," he said. "The lobster is legal in size but the way it was caught, is not. Throw it back."

Lobsters had been falling in and out of favor with humans since the dawn of man. At one point in history they were seen not as food, but bottom crawlers not unlike our present day cockroaches in terms of their appetite appeal. Scavengers of the seafloor.

On the way back into the harbor, they shared stories from the night dive. “Did you see the eel — it was glowing like a firefly”, “Bioluminescence… just imagine if we could harness all that energy”, “Did you know that over 5000 species of fish have bioluminescence?”, “Ya, and if they grow up near a power plant, multiply that times a million! Nothing like a little radioactivity to give a fish that nice soft glow.”

Natalie sat on the bow for the ride back, taking in the harbor with its commercial fishing fleets, aircraft carriers, cruise lines, and bobbing sailing ships with masts that teeter-tottered like a wheat field in the breeze. The reflections of downtown sparkled in the harbor and the Coronado Bridge stretched like a string of Christmas lights across the bay.

CHAPTER TWENTY-ONE
Tsukiji, Japan
February 20, 4 pm

A trail of longshoremen bustled in and out of every orifice of the huge vessel, like ants. The late afternoon sun projected them on the hull in long shadows that transformed them to 50-foot giants toiling away at the docks.

The *Initin* that was over 400 feet long, and was flying the Spanish flag. It had the capacity to carry 3,000 tons of tuna per trip. Its nets were the size of Manhattan.

The 3,000-ton capacity was double the local catch of some Pacific Island countries in a good year, and that number was dwindling fast. Foreign invasion of local fishing grounds had upset things to the point where many of these countries could no longer feed themselves. From the Maldives to the Channel Islands, artisan fishing boats were coming home empty. The *Initin* was among the most corrupt commercial operations, and it was targeted by the environmentalists. It was a symbol of how the fishing industry was destroying the entire food chain in the world's oceans. Greenpeace had stalked the shipyard and posted footage of its whole ghastly operation on You Tube. The Rainbow Warrior was known to follow it around and interrupt its nets. Most recently they had hung 100-foot *No Fish, No Future* banners on its hull in the Bering Sea. Who knows how many fish the *Initin* caught or brought in? No laws held them accountable. Greenpeace called these types of ships, destroyers. Today, the vessel loomed above the harbor like a monster intent on devouring every last fish in the sea.

Refrigerated ice trucks emerged bumper-to-bumper from the bowels of the ship to weight stations. The drivers took a number and proceeded to a ticket booth. Some kind of currency transaction took place with the attendant and they sped off to who knows where. Airports, warehouses, markets, canneries, food plants, cargo trucks, pharmaceutical labs, pet food factories, and cargo trains and other ships in the yard pulled up to giant cranes.

A crane twice as tall as the vessel was making vast sweeps that carried net upon net of wiggling fish from the ship's holding tanks to freight containers in the shipyard. Slowly the hull kept belching up fish until it floated higher in the water. Flapping in the wind, on the flagpole of the ship was now a new flag. Guatemala.

A stout white man wearing a hard hat and carrying a clipboard walked up the plank to the ship, where he was ushered into its belly. The vessel was a fishing boat, meatpacking plant, and floating cannery all in one. He walked around and inspected the hold. He was led by the ship's captain to a stairway leading to a vast compartment in the bilge which was stacked high with barrels of fishmeal, and cases of cans of tuna. Now, he began a ferocious negotiation.

"You don't have proper documentation. It is my liability," he barked at the captain.

The captain shot back at him, "I could have dumped them all out but I kept them for you."

"It brings you over your so-called-quota. Sell it for $2 million yen or I will turn you in, said the broker who moonlighted also as an inspector."

"Quota?" the captain laughed. "There is no QUOTA. We are flying under the flag of our choosing. People who talk about quotas find themselves lost at sea."

The buyer was a shrewd negotiator. "Oh, ya? Look, what is that?" He pointed to the sail bags hung on the ceiling of the hold, where only a ladder could reach them. A U.S. flag was spilling out of one of the stuffed bags. The buyer pointed back to the captain's face. "You won't get very far. We'll get you this time. This is illegal catch. Sell it to me for $2 million yen."

The captain's bodyguards armed with machine guns appeared at the steps. "Give me $2 million yen and go home," the boat captain said. "Come back tonight at midnight and we will unload them here." He pointed to some cranks on the side of hold. "With a barge. No lights. And no funny stuff."

The two men shook hands. The buyer tipped his hard hat to the armed guards and left the vessel the way he had come in.

CHAPTER TWENTY-TWO
Ocean Center Library
February 28, 10 am

Spar was at a table in the library flipping through the ocean chemistry section when Natalie noticed him and said hi. To this Spar replied, "Can you say fish sticks real fast 5 times? Fish sticks, fish sticks, fish sticks, fish sticks, fish sticks, fish sucks, fish ticks. Fish ticks?"

She wasn't laughing. "How you doing?" her friend asked. They'd both been at Ocean Center for eight years, though he had only begun as a student two years ago. Before that he was an aquarium hand.

"Let's see. How am I doing? Well, I defend my thesis to the review committee next week, giving me four more weeks to respond to their questions, then another three to rewrite it, make sure my margins are perfect, the pages are numbered, graphs are final, lines are double spaced and indexed, and the bibliography is as long as the Great Wall of China to prove that I've left no resource unturned. Meanwhile I have serious unresolved failures in my numbers."

"Ah, yes, and I have my own fish to fry. Try doing tracers on mercury. Let's take a break and swim the pier at lunch."

"Sorry I have to print out a draft of my entire thesis, over 200 pages so far, for a meeting with Jenkins and Salt. And the printer is down. They can send a man to the moon, a woman to the deepest trench on the ocean floor, but haven't yet made printers that don't jam."

Spar offered some sarcastic advice. "Just bend the curve back up." She knew he was kidding. "Or tell them the tuna population is in deep do-do, and it's not your fault. Which is probably accurate." He looked at her seriously this time. "Ask yourself if you are an activist, a capitalist or a politician? Or will you spend your doting years in the cozy embrace of a research institution, like the Mayan priests at Chichinitza who collected taxes from the peasants while sitting around predicting eclipses and making calendars?"

Natalie liked her brainy, nerdy friend, but sometimes she didn't know what the heck he was talking about. "You're so-o weird."

He was right about the activist thing. Already Sportfishing Weekly had called asking her to predict whether the supply of bluefin really was disappearing exponentially each day. She had made no comment. Then the reporter had asked her to make a statement about fish contamination and she had referred the lady to Spar.

"Did Sportfishing Weekly call you?" she asked him. Spar was already so deep in thought that he didn't hear her.

Natalie sat down at her computer and shot off an email to the taggers from Stanford asking for a tag data update. Then she sent one off to some folks she had met at the conference. "Please provide me an accurate account of the new quotas. Any new bycatch numbers? Ground up, dumped, or sold." SEND

She felt like she was caught in a global drama, far from the safe and cozy campus that she'd called home for eight years. Broken hearted, the innocence of scientific purism lost, and her parents fading.

Just then she remembered Sally's hair sample stored in an envelope in her purse. She left it on the table next to Spar with a note that read, "Can you test this for mercury?" He didn't even look up as he slipped it into his book bag. "Sure thing," he murmured on autopilot.

As she turned the corner, he called after her. "Did you know that plastic in the ocean has now outnumbered fish?"

Spar was known for his uncanny ability to store random data in his brain. When prompted, he would hypothesize why. Molecular-level memory encoding is postulated to include one or more changes to synaptic plasticity, constitution, connection, disconnection, gene expression, protein synthesis and phosphorylation, and probably other mechanisms that have yet to be discovered. Further, the method of encoding is likely different for the various levels of consolidation.

For the most part, Spar lived inside his head. He was an authentic genius and she appreciated their friendship.

CHAPTER TWENTY-THREE
Pt. Loma Navy Shipyard checkpoint
March 3, 7 pm

It was 7 pm by the time Natalie Scott and Jamie Robertson approached the military checkpoint to the North Island Naval Air Station Shipyard on Point Loma where the aircraft carriers were located. Jamie showed his military ID, and Natalie held up her civilian working papers, stamped with the Bottom Scratchers logo. "We're here to clean the hull of the big gray lady," Jamie said nodding to the aircraft carrier at the port.

The guard glanced at the Coast Guard parking permit on the dashboard of Jamie's blue Ford Escape and waved them through. They pulled up in front of the dock, parked the car, and begin to suit up in their scuba gear that consisted of wetsuit and hood, buoyancy compensator, tank, weights, regulator and gauge, compass, gloves, mask, headlamp, boots and fins.

Each checked the other's full rig and put knives in their sheaths. Natalie attached her knife handle to a thin fishing line secured to her weight belt.

“Why the fish line?” Jamie asked.

“I’ve dropped my knife almost one too many times. I nearly drowned six inches below surface last year, tangled in kelp. I didn’t panic, but untangling kelp from your neck when you can’t breathe and meanwhile you’ve dropped your knife can be very stressful. I almost wound up in Davy Jones’ Locker,” she said referring to the Bottom Scratcher’s expression for drowning.

“I can imagine,” said Jamie, impressed. “Learn something new every day.” She handed him some fish line and he secured his knife. “Huh, you learn something new every day.” He was looking at the waterline of the aircraft carrier, which indicated how deep the draft was at any time. When fully loaded, the water would be to the solid line that ran the circumference of the ship’s gray steel hull. The ship had only a 30-foot draft when empty, which it was. They’d have to do the waterline when it was fully loaded, another time. Poor planning. It's better to scrub a dub when it's fully loaded.

They reached for their battery-packed rotary scrapers with blades. These weed-wackers could peel growth off a boat hull like it was scotch tape. The aircraft carrier picked up all kinds of organisms in the furry growth it accumulated on its hull as it patrolled the world's oceans. It was a floating Navy base, fitted out like a small town with its own airport. It had eyes on the sky, and ears on the sea. With traffic on the high seas was getting busier than ever.

The ship played a part in evolution where invasive species were transported by humans from one sea to another, without an order of things. Without a plan. As a biologist, Natalie thought of ships as petri dishes. A very scary experiment that toyed with a complex ecosystem that nature had perfected for billions of years.

Al Stover had called Natalie at the last minute because the carrier had maneuvers to do and was only at port for a day or two. The decision to pull off the job at dusk was Natalie's because it was the only time Jamie was available to be her dive buddy, and he was the only dive buddy she could find. Besides, they had head lamps and evenings were safer because the docks were so busy by day. Divers ran the risk of getting run over by the shuttle boats to Coronado, or getting hit by equipment dropped overboard.

Underwater, they split up and started working top to bottom in vertical strips, sea grass falling off in big clumps through the army green water illuminated by their headlamps. With any luck, they'd get done both sides by midnight. That was at least $400 each.

They rose to the surface when the hull was as smooth as a billiard ball. Jamie's tank was almost out of air. Natalie about whom it was often remarked that she had gills, had a half tank left. Really it was because of her size and her calm, cool composure underwater where she felt most comfortable. Jamie took Natalie's scraper and swam it to the dockside, tying it off to a cleat. "Your harness, your highness?" he said referring to the magnetic harnesses they wore to hold them to the hull. "I've got it, but thank you," she said rolling it up and stuffing it in her BC, but taking note of his chauvinism. The good kind, not the bad kind.

They both inflated their BCs and just floated together in darkness gazing up at the stars for a while. "Maybe I was right," she said. "About what?" he asked. "I told Debby you were a gentleman." He sighed, "Guilty as charged… born and bred, m'am. By the way, where IS Debby?"

They could see the commercial fishing vessel where Roy worked, just down a few docks. It was all lit up making last minute preparations before it left port the next day. Helicopters were being secured to the deck to haul the prize fish off the boat in tanks while they were still breathing. Natalie imagined her roommate negotiating the ship in her heels. "Debby was invited to dreamboat's ship tonight for their last hurrah before he leaves."

Jamie didn't really want to envision this, and neither did Natalie. Roy seemed like a jerk.

He changed the subject. "Can you believe all that stuff living on the hull of the ship? It's like a whole microcosm. I wonder how many languages those critters speak?"

"Ya, there's probably a cure for some kind of disease growing under there and we killed it." He noticed that she looked genuinely sad at the thought. His heart skipped a little at her tenderness.

Then, Natalie's voice took on an unusual tone of mischief. "Hey, how about we go check the tuna boat's hull for the false-bottom mechanism that lover boy talked about. The jaw that opens and dumps the throwaways out before they reach port so they won't get caught over quota. Or if they're just plain *too dead* to be worth anything." At the conference, she heard rumors that supported the story that Roy he told at *The Pirate's Den.* They just keep filling the hull up and up, and dumping the old stuff out the bottom, all the way to port. They comb the seas for the cream of the crop, and let the other ones die. They get rid of them by gathering them into weighted nets that will sink to the bottom when they open the secret trap door, thus the name *false bottoms*.

Jamie cocked his head like a curious puppy. He was amused by the idea of scouting it out, but not sure he wanted anything to do with this caper. “Well, aren’t you the Nancy Drew detective? But more beautiful, like Katie Holmes. Do you think she’s related to Sherlock Holmes?” That was random, thought Natalie uncomfortably. She wanted to keep this professional and focused. Her eye was on the PhD.

The hull of the aircraft carrier was clean as a whistle, so their task was complete. Jamie thought about Natalie’s proposal to go check out Roy’s ship. “Let’s go find out if you’re right about the false bottom boat. But let’s stay close together, and when I say go, we go.” He held up his first two fingers, curled at the top like bunny ears hopping along. “This means *let’s go*.”

They talked about alibis. Their story would be that they were scraping down the carrier and got caught in the incoming tide. Both agreed they would take just a quick look and come right back without confrontation with the dock master. “So, Sherlock, if do you see any these trap doors, don’t push any knobs, levers or buttons, ok?” Jamie said. “Meanwhile, I’ll make sure the coast is clear while you nose around. Then we leave. You bang your tank with your knife if there is a problem.”

The two of them descended back into the dark water and swam off under the pilings toward the fishing vessel with their headlamps off. Once deep under the fishing vessel, Natalie shined her headlamp on the hull. Her eyes opened wide and a chill ran down her spine when she discovered an enormous jaw-like structure with a space age hinge that looked as though the whole bottom of the boat could yawn open like a belching monster. She took a very deep breath and let it out slowly. Roy, bless his pickled heart, was right. Natalie wondered, how many fish had they killed?

As planned, Jamie floated at about 10 feet below the surface on the look out for any trouble. His gaze swept the waters in the circumference of the ship. He entertained himself playing with a silvery bioluminescent needle-type fish that was swimming around his mask.

CHAPTER TWENTY-FOUR
The *S.S. Initin*, San Diego Harbor
March 6, 12 pm

Debby was on board the *Initin* with Roy. They were drinking straight from a bottle of champagne, and working their way through a labyrinth of partitions and watertight doorways on the way to his sleeping quarters. At some point she gave up on her heels, and carried them. The swaying of the ship made balancing on her six inch heals a feet feat. At his bunkroom, Roy swept her up in his arms and carried her over the rubber sealed doorway.

He had a nice room, all to his own that was befit for a man of some stature in the pecking order of the crew. Roy kissed her like there was no tomorrow, to make it last for the months he would be at sea. Still, she wasn't going all the way. She didn't want to wind up as some chump waiting for him to return and that's exactly what sex did to her. It made her imagine having the guy for keeps. For all she knew, there was a girl like her in every port.

"Where's the ladies room, baby?" she asked him, half trying to slow things down and to cool things off for a minute so she could keep her resolve.

Roy was pretty drunk by now. "Down the wall, I mean hull… hall. It has the sign of a mermaid on it. Don't fall in any portholes or potty holes or parabolas or whatever. And come right back. It's a jungle out there."

Debby went in search of the ladies room. On the way, she heard a strange sound coming from below. Then stop. Then she heard it again. Was someone locked in the ladies room? She followed the sound and found a door with a round glass window, sealed with an o-ring the size of a bike tire. Debby peered through. The vast bilge through the window reminded her of the story of Jonah inside the whale. It was the size of a football field but had ribs of steel. Curiously, the floor of the bilge was flat, not concave like the bottom of a boat. At one end, in a depression in the floor, was a gigantic rotor tiller with a chute on the side. It was the big fish grinder Roy had talked about. There was canning and packing equipment. At the bottom of a metal ladder was a big crank.

Suddenly, a security guard came up behind her, grabbed her elbow and pushed her against the closed door. "Go ahead, open it!" He pointed his gun at her head. "If you're so curious, open it, I said!"

Meanwhile up in the pilothouse of the vessel was an enormous control panel console that was right out of Star Trek. On a fish finder screen, divers could be seen. You could see one diver that appeared to be female nosing around the bottom of the vessel and another one, male, floating nearby playing with a fish. An angry pock-faced man stared at them in rage. "What in the world…? Get them!"

Back in the bilge, Debby was forced at gunpoint to climb down the ladder and crank the lever that opened the trap door to the false bottom of the boat. Seawater rushed in, flooding the bilge. Debby hung to the ladder in disbelief as the bottom of the boat all but disappeared leaving her staring at two scuba divers who were sucked into the hull.

The bigger one looked around, saw a gun pointed at them, and made a hopping bunny signal with his fingers to the other. They dove down and desperately kicked their fins to get out against the current. A true gentleman, Jamie motioned Natalie to go first.

The guard kept his gun aimed at Debby's head. "Close it. Now!!" The divers swam with all their might to get out the trap door before it closed. Meanwhile all the sonar beams and searchlights beneath the vessel went into full gear, illuminating the intruders.

"I can't," Debby screamed weak from fear. It's stuck!" At that, the security guard scrambled down the ladder. "Get in the water!"

Debby stared down in horror. "I can't swim." He grabbed a life ring from a hook on the hull and threw it in. "Good," yelled the security guard at Debby who had no choice but to jump. "I hope you drown."

He cranked the trap door shut catching one of Natalie's fins as she narrowly escaped. Jamie wasn't that lucky. He hovered at the bottom of the tank. A bullet shot by his head, and ricocheted off the thick steel hull, its deafening sound magnified a thousand times. Then there was another shot. He surfaced in surrender to find Debby, much to his surprise, floating in a life ring. "Debby, what are you doing in here?" he yelled. The security guard aimed his pistol at them both. "Shut up! Ok, now both of you come out."

The guard put a padlock on the crank, locking the hull shut again. He exited through the door with the big o-ring, and locked it shut too. Jamie and Debby sat on a stranded midpoint platform. Jamie wiggled out of his tank.

Up on the outside deck of the vessel, security guards with pistols stood in the shadows and peered over the side looking for the other diver. Powerful fishfinders scanned the water all around the boat. Light bounced off the bottom of the harbor, which was lit up like it was high noon.

The pock-faced man in the pilot room was trying to pick up a signal on Natalie but failed. “Prepare to disembark!” he announced into his walky-talky.

The *S.S. Initin* pulled in its lines, fired up the engines, and slipped into the darkness of the night, stealing out through the jetties. It was barreling toward the open seas beyond national jurisdiction. U.S. national jurisdiction, to be precise. Once in open water, the captain planned to pilot the ship south toward Mexico, with the help of the California Current.

CHAPTER TWENTY-FIVE
U.S. Navy shipyard, Pt. Loma
March 7, 8 am

Patrol officer Brady stood at the guard gate of the U.S. Navy Pt. Loma shipyard scratching his head. He was puzzled by the presence of a Ford Escape in the parking lot. Brady checked his roster and found that a vehicle with its license plate number had entered at seven pm the night before. It wasn't of great concern as military personnel came and went at all hours of the night in the shipyard. He could see a Coast Guard permit on the dash, and went over to take a look. Things looked pretty normal inside the car. Towels folded neat and orderly on the back seat. Two rucksacks, both men and women's he noted, seeing a brassiere strap dangling from one.

Brady decided to take a look around the lot. Officer Harguindeguy was just coming off the carrier and he stopped him. "Is there anyone left on the old gray mare, officer? I'm looking for the owner of that Ford Escape." He gave a military salute. "A Coast Guard officer."

"Not unless they're stowaways," he said. "The ship's on its way to maneuvers. It would have to be some pretty dumb stowaways!"

Brady thanked him with a salute and continued to patrol the lot. Funny, there were three empty scuba tanks along the seawall, plus one harness and two rotary boat-bottom scrapers. He walked up and down the wall, looking for clues as to whose car it might be. Back in his booth, he called the base.

"Officer Brady here, I need to get a read on the owner of Parking Permit #147-060. It appears to be Coast Guard."

The operator said. "The permit office is closed today. They cut it back to Tuesday, Thursday and Friday. Federal cutbacks. Try again tomorrow."

Brady looked back at the Ford Escape and scratched his head again. He got on the radio and called the Coast Guard.

CHAPTER TWENTY-SIX
The open sea
March 7, 8am

The *Initin* was beating it south at full throttle. To save her life, Natalie had attached herself with her emergency magnetic harness to the outside of the metal hull just beyond the perception of the searchlights and fish finder scanning equipment. She was sheltered from the eyes of the security guards on deck, and in between the ship's webcams. She had no choice but to hang on, or be shot by the guards. There was no turning back now, and letting go was not an option. Not way out there at sea. She saw Pt. Loma disappear into the distance.

CHAPTER TWENTY-SEVEN
The Coast Guard Station, Point Loma
March 7, 8 am

A Coast Guard alert was received on Channel 16. "It looks like we've got a missing person, a Lieutenant James L. Robertson. There's evidence that he and one of the Bottom Scratchers were last seen entering the Navy shipyard to clean the hull of the carrier at the dock. Their equipment is still sitting there. Do you read me?"

In minutes, Coast Guard defender boats swarmed into action while divers began searching beneath the aircraft carrier which they noticed polished to perfection. "Well, they were here anyway," the voice reported.

They spread out all over San Diego Harbor from the shipyard to Shelter Island, to Coronado and Imperial Beach looking for any clues as to where the divers could be.

Coast Guard helicopters began searching overhead. One of these sky hawk pilots named Buddy had heard the radio call and mentioned that the other diver may have been a Bottom Scratcher. He put a call into Al Stover, who had begun his career in the Coast Guard as a diving instructor. *His* diving instructor. Al's good-natured voice was on the machine, "Dive locker! Leave a message and I'll get right back to you, but don't hold your breath." Beep!

Buddy left a message. "Al, it's Buddy, U.S. Coast Guard. I'm looking for information on a Bottom Scratcher who may have scraping down the carrier at Pt. Loma last night. Call me back. Try Channel 16 first." Then, he called some of the other Bottom Scratchers he knew. It didn't take long for word to spread that one of their members was missing. Within the hour, there were divers everywhere, from Fish and Wildlife, the Park Service, dive clubs, and Navy Seal teams. With the tide now funneling quickly out between the jetties, it was a dangerous situation over which no one could get control.

Soon, an old familiar voice came over Buddy's radio. It was Al, radioing from the pier where he and Doug Jenkins had been messing around with some surf zone survey equipment. "Buddy, what's going on? I heard some commotion over the radio about some missing divers."

Captain Buddy Rodgers didn't want to alarm everybody until he had more information. "There is a Coast Guard lieutenant named Robertson missing, but we can't be sure if he is still in the water. His Ford Escape was found in the lot this morning. They also found two rotary scrapers on the wall, plus three empty tanks. The night guard said a Bottom Scratcher was with him."

It was Natalie, thought Al. "It's Natalie Scott," Stover said. Jenkins looked up in astonishment, "Natalie's missing?" He was pretty sure that wherever she was, she would show up the next day for her presentation to her thesis advisors at 5 pm. She wouldn't miss it for the world. Stover tended to agree. Besides, she was one of the best divers he knew. It would be strange if she'd had a diving accident. But, still something was wrong. The empty tanks. The scrapers. The car.

CHAPTER TWENTY-EIGHT
Rio de Janeiro
March 7, 10 am

It was 2 am when Domingo's phone began vibrating in his pocket on the dance floor in the disco district of Rio. But he didn't notice. He was entangled in the samba with a flamenco dancer, gyrating to the heavy beat of club music. When he awoke the next morning, there were ten messages from his boat captain. He listened to the last message first, which was all he needed to hear. Domingo shook the girl who was in his bed and told her to leave. He shoved her out the door with her clothes, while stuffing money in her hand. He rushed downtown to his glass tower. By 10 am he was squinting in disbelief at his computer screen, replaying footage over and over again of some snooping idiots who were caught diving around one of his ships that was holding over in San Diego.

"What happened to the second diver? Who ARE these people?" he hollered into the phone, pounding on his desk.

The boat captain of the *Initin* told him again and again the same thing he had been telling him for the last twenty minutes. "She disappeared from the imaging equipment and we think she got away. That is, unless we ran her over. We have one of her fins. Size small." The captain chuckled a little bit at that.

Why did this guy have to make a joke out of everything? If he wasn't one of the best captains on the high seas with the worst moral compass, Domingo would have fired him a long time ago just for his bad jokes. He could never get a straight answer from the guy.

"Well, what did she see?"

"Like I said, I don't know what she saw."

"You've got $50 million dollars of equipment on that vessel and you can't pick up on a goddam scuba diver in 20 feet of water? There's someone out there swimming around with one flipper who may have enough information to sink our whole operation and you don't know where she is? Why don't you put your thinking cap on and go ask your other captives? Then, grind ‘em up and spit ‘em out. No, that might leave evidence. Sink ‘em!” He punctuated the end of the conversation by slamming a fist down on the phone which ended the call.

CHAPTER TWENTY-NINE
San Diego Harbor
March 7, 10 am

Back at the Navy yard, Officer Brady had broken into the Ford Escape. He found the Bottom Scratcher documents of Natalie Scott. He also found her iPhone. He was looking for any clue as to where they might have gone. One by one, he listened to her messages. Her father. Her father. Her father. Debby. He listened to Debby's message. "Hey Nat, it's me Deb. Roy and I had dinner at *The Pirates Den* and then went to the boat for a farewell party because he's leaving tomorrow. I might not be home tonight. Love ya." The rest of the messages were all from the girl's father.

He pressed the *return call* button and got Debby's machine. No luck there. Listening to Mr. Scott's calls, it was obvious that the girl's father didn't know where she was either.

Officer Brady watched the drama unfolding around him as the San Diego Harbor filled to the brim with search parties that had come from everywhere from Chula Vista to El Cajon, and from all the way up in Oceanside to look for the missing divers. It was a zoo. TV stations were circling the shipyard in helicopters. News of the missing divers was on every channel.

The Pirates Den didn't answer so he motored over there in the skiff and banged on the door. Lucy the day manager let him in. The place was a local hangout and they knew each other. "Lucy, did you have a reservation for a guy named Roy last night?" Lucy shook her head. "Santorini doesn't need a reservation. He's a regular. That's his skiff, *Time Out*, right there."

"Do you know where they went? We are trying to find his date Debby to talk to her. Her roommate is missing. This Debby girl might have been with this Roy character last night."

"Look deary, Roy is Roy. He comes to port, has a good time and then goes back to sea. He was leaving today so I wouldn't be surprised if last night, you know, he had a lady friend with him on the boat and stayed out late."

Brady looked at the *Time Out.* You couldn't have much of a farewell party on that small boat.

"She said she was going to a boat. Was there any other boat?" Brady knew this was a long shot. This Debby girl, even if he could find her, probably didn't know where her roommate was.

"Roy took a job with a tuna fleet when he and his brother folded up their sport fishing business. Call his brother, Luke. No he's in Panama. Look, I got to get back to work." She led him to the door. "Good luck finding the roommate." On second thought she called after him and pointed toward Pier 84, the largest commercial pier in the harbor, not counting the cruise ship launch. "There was a big one with the flag from, like, I don't know, Mexico or somewhere."

"Was it Guatemala?"

"It could have been Peru, Chile or Kalamazoo! I don't know the difference. If it's not our stars and stripes, they all look the same to me. Look,

I gotta go. I hope you find what you're looking for."

Brady hopped back in the skiff and passed by Pier 84, which was empty. He called Todd, the harbormaster. "Todd, where's that big tuna boat that was here?"

Todd looked up the dock reservations. "Let's see. Carnival Cruise is leaving today. Booze Cruise is doing a day trip for gamblers, the carrier's leaving for maneuvers. Oh, the *Initin* is supposed to be leaving later today."

Brady looked at the empty slip. He wouldn't have missed a 500-foot floating cannery vessel passing by with satellite dishes and helicopters on it. Brady said, "Well, it's gone." Todd marked the boat as gone in the books, which meant there was opening at Pier 84. At $100 per foot per night, Pier 84 was a cash cow. He thought about the loss of income if *Initin* had truly left early. Odd that they didn't even fuel up, he thought.

Brady paid the pier a visit. There were lots of sketchy deckhands standing around who had, literally missed the boat. A Cisco shipping container was there with boatload of food and supplies with the same problem. Brady called the Coast Guard and got a vessel number on the *Initin*. Interesting, it had more than one registration number. One registered to Guatemala. Another to Uruguay. Another to Venezuela. Russia. Chile. Nothing was making any sense.

The deckhands were all lying around, passed out. They were most likely Shanghai'd from bars the night before. It was an expression used for kidnapping unsuspecting patrons who were so drunk they didn't know what happened until they woke up at sea as indentured servants with no escape. The practice began in Shanghai, China where there was a shortage of boat laborers.

CHAPTER THIRTY
Off the coast of San Diego
March 7, 10 am

Roy woke up with a fuzzy hangover and another odd sensation. It felt like the ship was underway. He looked out his portal and saw nothing but a blue horizon. This confused him and he tried to recollect the night before. Pirates Den, check. Picking up champagne, check. Carrying Debby over the threshold, check. Making out, check. He couldn't remember anything after that. He looked at his watch and tried to figure out what day it was. Still in a drunken stupor, he saw the high-heels on the floor. "She stood me up," he muttered.

Meanwhile, down in the bilge the guard was prodding Debby and Jamie toward the chute into the fish grinder to be canned as cat food. "Who was the other diver?" he demanded. He stopped to take a call on his radio. Heeding new instructions, he opened the door to a small closet with a control panel. A massive net dropped from above and soon Debbie and Jamie were caught in the snare, dangling from the cables.

Slowly the bottom of the boat yawned open wide suspending the captives over a gaping hole that was open to the sea bottom, 3500 feet below. “Who was the other diver?” he demanded

The security guard lowered the net a little more. Debby had no idea who the other diver was. Frankly she hadn’t a clue what Jamie Robertson was doing there. “I don’t know, she cried! I was just here on a date!” The guard lowered the net a little more. “The other diver was Natalie Scott,” Jamie said quietly surrendering to the fact there was little they could do to escape at this point. Debby looked at him in horror. “Were you spying on me,” she cried. “Hardly,” said Jamie. I was just as surprised to see you as you were to see me.”

Jamie didn’t know if Natalie had been shot or not. But the security guard’s sudden interest in her gave him hope that she was still at large. Maybe even getting help. But by the looks of things, it would be too late for Debby and him. The guard thanked him very much for offering up Natalie’s identity. He smiled with a sinister, toothy grin that sparkled with gold crowns.

Then, he took out a massive sword and cut the line, dropping the net that held his captives into Davy Jones' locker.

Jamie thrashed at the net with his knife as they sank through the ship's false bottom trap door, slowly into the sea.

Meanwhile, Natalie was still clinging for life to the outside of the hull in her magnetic harness. She'd heard screaming through the hull and thought she heard the crank again. The ship had come to a halt for a moment. The bottom of the hull opened wide beneath her position. She saw a net being lowered. She looked underwater to see what it could be. She thought she saw people. Natalie put her regulator in her mouth, grabbed her knife and chased it as fast as she could with only one fin.

She slashed at the net, dropping her knife, which dangled by its safety line. That's when she saw Debby clawing at the net with her long nails. As she ducked out of the way of the net, she came face to face with her roommate, whose eyes grew wide. What was she doing here?

Jamie was slashing their way out when he dropped his own knife. Dangling by its fish line, he groped at it. In seconds he and Natalie were face to face slashing at the net together. Just in time they escaped as Natalie pulled them through the net and they escaped. She grabbed them both by the arms, inflated her vest, and the three of them bobbed to the surface gasping for air, just as the net dropped out of sight to the bottom of the sea.

Looking up, there was no blue sky. Unfortunately, they had bobbed back up into the holding tank, and the jaw of the trap door was closing again. “Dive” screamed Jamie. “I can’t swim!” Debby sputtered. “Well, you’re about to get a crash course in scuba diving,” cried Natalie. “Put this in your mouth and just breathe. Hold me tight,” she told her friend. She stuck her octopus rig in Debby’s mouth as Jamie forced the air out her buoyancy compensator.

He powered both of the girls down to the closing trap door. Just before it closed, he pushed them out. With all the exertion, he couldn't hold his breath any longer, and he fell behind.

Surfacing again in the hull, Jamie scurried up the ladder to reverse the crank and the gap began to open again. His scuba gear was still sitting on the mid-platform of the ship's ribs. He grabbed it and jumped back in the hold to escape through the gap. Just then, the guard returned, outraged to see that this pain in the ass was still alive. At least there was only one left. The other one was surely shark bait by now.

The guard fired up the fish grinder. It created a huge eddy current that whirled around the bilge like a giant toilet being flushed. Jamie was quickly getting sucked into the chute that fed the monster. He made every effort to swim against it but was no match for the machine that could suck up 3000 tons of tuna in one meal.

As he approached the teeth of the chute he could see the spinning blades. Just in time he shoved his tank into the fish grinder's mechanism and it exploded, bringing the machine to a screeching halt. He grabbed his knife, cut its line and aimed it at the guard. With the precision of a dart to the dartboard, he hit the guard right between the eyes. Bull's eye! As the guard toppled from the platform, Jamie scrambled up the ladder to grab his pistol.

It was then that Jamie noticed a collection of tuna tags like the ones in Natalie's lab, displayed on the wall like trophies. He ripped one off the wall and stuffed it in his vest.

CHAPTER THIRTY-ONE
Sally's house, Oceanside
March 7, 3 pm

Natalie's sister Sally was home from work and had parked the kids in front of the TV. Their program was interrupted by the news with a breaking story delivered by anchorwoman Paula Zone. "A marine biologist and a lieutenant in the U.S. Coast Guard have been kidnapped by a tuna boat," the reporter announced to the world. "The Coast Guard has spotted the vessel and is now engaged in a high-speed chase. A U.S. Navy destroyer had been dispatched and is barreling south from Long Beach and an aircraft carrier has been deployed from San Diego."

The TV screen showed a satellite image of a 500-foot fishing vessel off the coast of Mexico. Helicopters were hovering above the vessel like black flies. The footage cut to an armada of Coast Guard boats speeding to the scene. The fishing boat was zigzagging back and forth in and out of U.S. and international waters. The biologist gone missing and assumed to be onboard was identified as Natalie Scott.

"Natalie!" screamed Sally at the television in horror. "It's Aunt Natalie!"

Back on the Vineyard, Mr. Scott had his headphones on. He had been trying to reach Natalie ever since Sunday night. At home, in the lab, and on her cellphone. Even the receptionist hadn't picked up the phone and he was getting anxious. He knew that her big moment to stand before her advisory committee and present her thesis was 5 pm Pacific Standard Time the next day. Mr. Scott was trying to reach his daughter to wish her luck.

CHAPTER THIRTY-TWO
S.S. Initin
March 7, 3 pm

The GPS chart in the control panel of the *Initin's* pilothouse plotted the vessel as it drifted back and forth over the boundary from national to international waters beyond jurisdiction, known as the high seas. Once in the high seas, it was no man's land where gangsters and thieves ruled, though ocean advocates had been tirelessly campaigning at the United Nations to create governance.

So far, neither the Coast Guard nor the *Initin* had opened fire. The Coast Guard had managed to hook the vessel with a line and engage in a tug of war to keep the *Initin* in U.S. waters until back up arrived. The Coast Guard boats were dwarfed in size and no match for a 500-foot trumped up multi-million-dollar high-tech fishing vessel that was catching and grinding up nearly everything in its path.

"Cut the goddam line!" screamed the fishing captain in Portuguese, pointing at the rope. "Free us from those wimpy little bastards before I lose my temper and sink every last one of them."

The *Initin* carried enough ammunition on board to the sink the entire British Armada. It had refrained from deploying weapons lest they start World War III. The captain had been given strict orders not to damage the mother ship for insurance reasons, and not to open fire. If the *Initin* opened fire, it would be a shot heard round the world and retaliation could be costly to the vessel. Besides, this had now become an international story on every website and news channel on the planet. Satellite cameras in outer space were documenting the whole thing. They were under a microscope.

The Coast Guard wasn't anxious for a battle at sea, either. It didn't stand a chance until the U.S. destroyer arrived. They stood off, getting dragged by the *Initin* deeper and deeper into international waters.

Coming over the blue horizon they could see that the Greenpeace Rainbow Warrior was closing in on them.

CHAPTER THIRTY-THREE
Rio de Janeiro
March 7, 4 pm

Domingo was watching the drama unfold on video cameras and TV monitors in his office, including a satellite image with coordinates superimposed over a GPS plot map. "Gun it! You're drifting, you idiot," he screamed at the captain.

He called his lobbyist lawyer in Washington, who was a dominant force in preventing any kind of high seas alliance from putting restrictions on the free-for-all that was the high seas. The high seas were his! He owned every frigging thing from top to bottom if he could catch it. That's how he looked at it. In the name of Ocean Enterprises, Salvador Rodriguez Domingo had poured millions of dollars into paying off politicians to veto anything that limited their right to pillage the seas. It was time for pay back!

"According the North American Free Trade Agreement as long as we stay 100 miles from

U.S. soil, we have every right to be in those waters, and they can't search us. So tell your fancy Senator friend to call off the dogs or we'll happen to mention his cannery business in Belize. He can also forget about any campaign support in the future from Ocean Enterprises. Then, call that snitch in Taiwan. Tell him that we're not going to set the nets for another week. They can eat dog meat for all I care."

Just then, there was the sound of an explosion on the ship coming from deep in the bilge so loud that it was picked up on his speakerphone. "What the hell was that?" he yelled at the captain shaking his head so hard that his hair shook out of place.

CHAPTER THIRTY-FOUR
Off the coast of California
March 7, 3 pm

The shaking fear of drifting into the sea unnoticed fueled a rush of adrenalin so powerful that Natalie found the strength to attach Debby to the metal hull with her magnetic harness. She held on to her roommate for dear life.

The girls were both at risk of losing their grip. The weight of them together was making the harness give way to gravity. It kept slipping down below the surface as Natalie kept repositioning the magnets. She held the regulator in Debby's mouth so she could breathe. "Breathe," she said. "Breathe." Between breaths, Debby was screaming and waving frantically at the Coast Guard cutters and helicopters to no avail. They still had not spotted the girls sandwiched in the middle of it all. The girls could see all the action, but could do nothing.

CHAPTER THIRTY-FIVE
NOAA Headquarters
March 7, 4 pm

The National Oceanic and Atmospheric Administration headquarters was on the phone with NASA. They were monitoring the scene unfolding off the coast of California. A U.S destroyer was steaming south from Long Beach from the north, and helicopters were swarming out of San Diego. At the center of the whole thing was the *S.S. Initin*, struggling to stay 100 miles offshore against a fleet of U.S. Coast Guard cutters that had managed to hook the ship and were tugging it back to national waters. The whole mess was floating south toward Mexico. It was a multinational tug of war. From space, it looked like an entangled mess of ocean debris.

All eyes were on the screens as the strange entanglement snaked back and forth over the international boundary, beyond which anarchy and piracy ruled the sea.

Suddenly, the fishing vessel raised its towering cranes and cast a net out over the whole Coast Guard fleet.

A Coast Guard helicopter got its propeller caught in the net and crashed to the deck. Now the entire force was immobilized.

CHAPTER THIRTY-SIX
U.S. Initin
March 7, 3:00 pm

Natalie, in her wet suit, and Debby, in her little black dress, clung like refrigerator magnets to the hull of the ship. Oddly, Natalie was thinking of her brother Finn. How he must have felt the moment he died. Did he think of the people who loved him that he was leaving behind?

Above them, the girls saw the towering metal arm of a crane that was casting a net from the ship out over the U.S. Coast Guard fleet.

Natalie saw it as their big chance to escape. “Deb, we’re going to let go and swim or crawl over to the Coast Guard. It’s now or never. Keep the regulator in your mouth and breathe slowly and calmly to conserve the air. We’re going to need it. Think yoga.” Debby was pretty much hyperventilating. “Yoga? Are you crazy?” she said. Natalie remained cool. “Ok, much calmer than you are breathing now. In, and out. In and out. Like this.” Natalie demonstrated how to breathe into the regulator. “Now, put it in your mouth. Breathe. Here we go. Just breathe and hold on to me."

They slipped out of the magnetic harness and the two of them held hands and descended into the cold Pacific Ocean to about 35 feet deep, and then swam beneath the net to the nearest Coast Guard boat, staying out of sight.

Once on the far side of the first boat, they slowly ascended to the surface. At the surface, Natalie inflated her vest. The two of them bobbed by the side of the boat and looked for something to grab onto. "Ok, Deb, now you can start screaming!" Which she did.

A female officer, Caroline Evans, was on deck slashing at the huge gill net that had enveloped the fleet. She looked over the rail and much to her surprise saw two girls bob up from the depths of the sea.

In moments, Evans deployed a life raft over the side that inflated upon impact. Natalie pushed freezing Debby into the raft, ditched her tank, and climbed in herself. The raft was hauled up to the vessel, and pulled up onto the deck that was in mass chaos under the net. They were wrapped in thermal blankets and rushed off the deck and into the galley.

“You wouldn’t happen to be Natalie Scott would you?” Evans asked. “And you must be Debby.”

Evans gave them both a big burly hug, fighting back the urge to cry. She reached out to shake Natalie’s hand.

“What’s the matter with your hand?” she asked, seeing blood. For the first time, Natalie noticed that Debby had clawed her hand to the bone with her nails. Natalie was just glad to be alive. “Just a little scratch.”

Meanwhile press boats were arriving at the scene despite warnings to stay back. While waiting onboard for updates, TV correspondent Paula Zone was biding her time by interviewing foreign diplomats via Skype. Could shortages of fish be starting a war? Had they been up for grabs for way too long?

Soon, CNN, ESPN, Fox, NBC and CBS helicopters were hovering in the air all around them. Their footage afforded those on both boats to see a bird's eye view of themselves on TV and they stared in disbelief. The net cast by the *Initin* was so big and had been cast so far, even the widest angle cameras couldn't take it all in. Satellite imagery from NASA showed a huge entangled flotilla being towed by the *Initin* further out to sea and south toward Mexico, as news teams circled above.

The recovery of Natalie and Debby had not hit the airwaves yet and the Coast Guard crew had strict orders not to talk to the press.

CHAPTER THIRTY-SEVEN
Martha's Vineyard
March 7, 9 pm EST

Herman Scott had been watching the news ever since Sally called him and told him to turn on the TV.

Newscasters on every station were updating the public. Cameras had footage of the *Initin* which had just cut loose from the enormous net the ship had cast over the Coast Guard fleet. The vessel was now severed from the fleet which was still caught in the net. Untethered, it was gunning it for the high seas. They were beating it west and then south toward Mexico as fast as they could go.

Barreling down on the *Initin* was the Navy destroyer from the north. Fighter planes from the aircraft carrier, and a swarm of helicopters looked like bees driven from a hive chasing its prey. The fleet of Coast Guard cutters were snipping their way out of the net, methodically disentangling themselves.

Then, Herman Scott thought he saw a blurry shot of his daughter Natalie emerge from the mess of nets wrapped in a blanket. Two figures were getting hoisted from into a small rescue hammock dangling from a Coast Guard helicopter.

"Look, Margaret, it's Natalie! I'll bet she found those fish!"

Cameras followed the helicopter back to a heliport on the aircraft carrier. From there he could see two girls in fatigues hustled on to a fighter jet. The news channels followed the jet for twenty minutes to the San Diego airport where an ambulance was waiting among throngs of people who had gathered for the spectacle.

CHAPTER THIRTY-EIGHT
Lindbergh Field, San Diego Airport
March 7, 6 pm

At Lindbergh Field, San Diego's airport, both girls protested the ambulance that was waiting for them. They were fine, but for some minor scrapes. In fact, they were both in surprisingly good condition. Caroline Evans had given them dry clothes, and hot food.

Debby and Natalie knew less than the general public about what was going on. They were trying to understand. Debby asked, "Do you think Jamie is alive and still on the ship?" This was the million-dollar question that they couldn't answer or do anything about at the moment. "Well, the whole U.S. military is looking for him, so if he is alive, they'll find him. There's nothing we can do but listen to the news like everybody else."

When the two girls saw the stampede of reporters storming toward them across the tarmac, they jumped quickly into the ambulance. Still in shock, Natalie and Debby both had the same idea at the exact same time. "Let's get out of here," they said together. Debby looked down at the Coast Guard fatigues. "Ya, I don't want to be seen on TV dressed like this!" She leaned over to the driver. "Can we slip away from here… under the radar?"

"Good idea." He flipped on the blinking lights, stepped on the gas, and aimed for the service exit, but didn't get very far before they were surrounded by media trying to get a statement. Blocking their path, reporters and photographers crowded around the windows shouting and snapping pictures. "Do you know where Lieutenant Robertson is?" "What were you doing on that fishing vessel?" "Were you kidnapped?" In an instant the faces of Natalie and Debbie were plastered all around the world.

The driver cranked up the siren, and sped away to take them home. As they came down over Point Loma into Ocean Beach, he finally slowed down and turned to them, still not sure where to go. "Have you seen the television?" He turned on the vehicle's flatscreen TV and found a news channel.

A newsreel cut to a headline that read, *Stowaways or Kidnapped?* An anchorwoman came on camera. "Two San Diego girls, one presumably a bluefin tuna fisheries biologist from the Ocean Center who was investigating illegal fishing activities, and the other her roommate who was presumably on a date with a deckhand, were rescued from the ship of a large-scale fishing operation by the U.S. Coast Guard today off the coast of southern California. The question this hour is, where is Coast Guard Lieutenant James Robertson, also missing? Meanwhile, calls made to the fishing ship's owner of record, Ocean Enterprises, to which the vessel is registered, have not been returned."

The news stations began getting comments from anyone they could find. Lucy at *The Pirate's Den*, Al and the Bottom Scratchers, Friends of the River, drinking buddies from the Gaslamp district and anyone else they could find who would talk. One of those people was Chad who was going on and on about Natalie and her research, slipping up and referring to her as his wife a few times, just to get interviewed.

They even got a few words out of Spar. "I have no doubt that she was up to something, and that something was most likely the scientific study of Pacific bluefin."

Sally and her three kids were on camera dressed in the new Ralph Lauren winter yachting collection. Sally took the spotlight, broadcast out across the world on every channel as she spoke about her sister's research and the dangers of mercury in the fish. "I'm just so grateful my sister is alive." The cameras got cute shots of the kids. "Aunt Natalie was looking for her fish, I think," "No, she got kidnapped by some bad people I think." "I want to ride in the helicopter too." "I said it first!" "No you didn't, I did."

Back on their living room, Mr. and Mrs. Scott were mesmerized by what they saw on the television, yet confused by the whole thing. Margaret said, "Why is Sally on the television with Natalie's children? Oh, look, there's Chad!" With the kindness of a saint, her husband gently corrected her. "Those are Sally's kids, Margaret. Natalie doesn't have any children." Margaret thought long and hard about this. “Well, what is she waiting for?”

The girls sat stunned in the back of the ambulance trying to put the pieces together themselves. Then, Natalie noticed the time. It was almost 7 pm. “Take a right,” she said when they got to Sunset Cliffs. “We’re going to La Jolla.”

CHAPTER THIRTY-NINE
SS Initin
March 7, 4 pm

The captain of the *Initin* had still not gotten word of the rescue and was feeling pretty smart. For all he knew, they had dunked the snooping passengers, killing any evidence of foul play in the bilge of the boat. As he crossed the Mexican border ahead of the U.S. destroyer, he cheered.

He was so happy with himself that he called his boss to leave him a message. "Did you see that Salvador? We just crossed the border. If they try to touch us now, it would be World War III. I guess you could say we dodged a bullet." Then he realized that he was talking into voicemail. "Salvador?"

Domingo had packed his bags and was heading to a small, private airport, making one stop at the bank. He'd thrown away his cell phone so he couldn't be traced. The gravity of the series of events was not lost on him. He'd been watching the whole drama unfold on networks all over the world in every language. He'd recognized the face of Natalie Scott, that broad at the conference. What was she doing nosing around his boat?

The *Initin* was now flying the Mexican flag and heading to Ensenada to fuel up. Back off the west coast of Mexico, just on the horizon, the captain could see the Greenpeace Rainbow Warrior getting closer. He radioed a sister ship to get rid of them.

Just then he saw a reflection in the control panel that looked like a gun pointed at his head. He looked up to see the face of Lieutenant Jamie Robertson, who was already roping him to the pilot seat and tightening the knots.

"Turn the ship around. Now."

CHAPTER FORTY
Ocean Center
March 7, 7:15 pm

Most of the scientists and researchers at the Ocean Center had collected around the TV monitors in the auditorium where PhD candidate Natalie Scott had been scheduled to present the preliminary findings for her thesis *"Trends and predictions in the Pacific Bluefin Tuna populations."* Her advisory board was all there discussing the ramifications of the situation.

None of them noticed the spinning red ambulance light that lit up the campus like a disco ball.

As a hush came over the room, they looked up to see Natalie slip in and step up to the podium, still wearing Coast Guard fatigues.

"Friends, colleagues, and esteemed advisors, I am pleased to present preliminary findings for my PhD thesis: *"Trends and predictions in the Pacific Bluefin Tuna populations."*

Upon conclusion, Natalie asked if there were any questions. There were quite a few. Enough to keep the discussion going well past midnight and into the next morning. And then again the next day. And the next. Until Natalie was confident in her ability to characterize the present and predict the future of this marvelous marine creature if everybody got on board to save it.

Already, great changes were being made in Pacific bluefin tuna management, from the top down, and from the bottom up. People everywhere were taking a stand for conservation until the fish stocks recovered. Diners were asking chefs to please take it off the menu. Seafood markets stopped seeing bluefin as food, but as a species with rights of its own.

An avalanche of stories and legends came out about bluefin, and artists were choosing these amazing athletes of the deep as subject matter. An open source repository of data was created by citizen scientists to monitor seaports and fish markets for illegal catches. Sport fishermen took it upon themselves to protect the juveniles and toss them back into the great blue frontier which they had called home for over 50 million years.

CHAPTER FORTY-ONE
Marine Biology Lab
April 29, 3 pm

Natalie was printing out graphs and charts. The sun had come up, reached high noon and begun to set again. The signature page was sitting on her desk, all signed. She placed the final signed PhD thesis in her book bag, and began the long, steep trek to upper campus.

In the graduate administration office, it was nearly 4 pm and Betty Stolz was just locking up when she saw Natalie Scott pulling on the door frantically while pounding on the glass in a frenzy.

Betty came to the door and looked at her, eye to eye, with no expression at all. Natalie's heart sank. Refresher courses, she thought. After all that. She pulled and pulled on the door. Betty was saying something assumed to be, "we're closed." Natalie just stared at her in disbelief that anyone could be so cruel? She kept pulling on the door till she'd almost pulled the handle off.

Betty pointed to a sign on the door and mouthed out the words, "Push!"

CHAPTER FORTY-TWO
The Auditorium
May 25, 9am

The poster outside the small auditorium read, *Trends and Predictions in Pacific Bluefin Tuna Populations"by doctorate candidate Natalie Scott.*

In the front row were Margaret and Herman on one side of the aisle. Members of the advisory board were seated in the front row of the other side. Salt and Jenkins were at the podium coaching Natalie. This was the last hurdle. She still could be stumped by a question from the board during her final oral presentation, so it wasn't quite over yet.

Debby was seated behind the Scott family, nestled between Jamie and Spar. Faculty and students were filing into the room and filling up the seats. Then came Al Stover and other members of the Bottom Scratchers. Then came Coast Guard officers Evans and Brady. There was Rebecca from the food chain group. Lily from reception. Lucy from *The Pirates Den*, and divers from all over San Diego County. They filled the room until it was standing room only. Chad and his girlfriend were standing in the back row having some kind of argument until she finally stormed off.

Natalie took the podium and began her presentation, projecting the graphics from her thesis onto the big screen.

"A dramatic shift in ocean circulation is set off at the poles where melting ice caps are creating new currents that affect the direction and depth of the migratory patterns of large pelagic fish. Enormous changes in the salinity, density, depth and direction of the currents can be attributed to the spike in the earth's temperature as carbon emissions from our fossil fuel consumption trap heat from the sun. Global warming is not a matter of if, but a matter of how much it will take for the entire circulation of the world's oceans to adjust to the new climate. The slightest shift in wind patterns and temperature are magnified beneath the sea. Our climate is governed by the sea, and the sea is governed by the climate. We know that thermo-regulating, warm-blooded bluefin are capable of adapting, and they probably are. My theory is that every fish in the food chain will be altering its migratory pattern. We don't have a read on the new routes. It's like a new traffic plan and it's happening quickly. Feeding, breeding and spawning areas will change, their food source will change.

But one thing will remain constant. Our vigilant protection of the species. Unfortunately, they are not traveling beyond the perception of the commercial fishing industry's highly sophisticated tracking technology.

Natalie continued to explain that what was once subsistence fishing in the great ocean, the global common, had become the gold mine of a vast complex, ungoverned and illegal commercial fishing industry. Floating canneries the size of a city block were grinding up everything within their reach, before they ever touched land. Slave workers were kidnapped and dumped at sea for insubordination. False bottom boats were dumping nets of dead fish out the bowel in a cat and mouse game with fish markets. The vendors of multi-national conglomerates were using rogue scientists to find tagged fish leading them to feeding grounds. Natalie explained that suddenly man was killing off much more Pacific bluefin than any of them could ever have imagined, or that the data could predict. Babies were served as sushi. Man had nearly taken the population to the point of no return. Even her tuna tag project had been hacked!

But now satellite data could track vessel traffic on the sea every four days, and the latest in pattern recognition systems can now decipher whether they are fishing, shipping, studying, snooping or attacking.

It wasn't just over fishing, it was over sifting. "Imagine the entire ocean sifted through nets 20 miles wide and 2000 feet deep," she continued. The screen filled with doom and gloom.

Finally, she offered a glimmer of hope. But it wasn't just one glimmer of hope. It was a string of protected areas for ocean wildlife restoration called Hope Spots. Natalie showed a global map highlighting carefully selected marine protected areas that encircled the ocean with Hope Spots like a string of pearls. She had calculated how long it would take to bring the Pacific bluefin populations back to a healthy state again by protecting spawning, feeding and breeding sites. Natalie then drew two extreme scenarios, where the population could make a comeback under certain conditions, or drop off to zero if nothing was done right away.

As her final slide, she revealed a graph that depicted a rise in the Pacific bluefin population if the killing stopped. It curved up, and soared into the future.

"Now I'll be happy to take your questions," she said with confidence.

After being drilled by her committee for a good hour, there were no more questions. She thanked each and every member of the committee, and then sat down.

Her dad got up and clapped. Everyone followed.

Dr. Jenkins took the podium. "Thank you, Miss Scott. Please be patient while the review com-

mittee draws its own conclusion about your candidacy for a Doctorate in Marine Biology having completed your verbal dissertation."
The review committee and the faculty of the Ocean Center passed its votes down to Dr. Jenkins who tallied them up.

One by one they signed the final master diploma. Then, everyone in the audience jumped up to congratulate her. Dr. Jenkins turned to the audience. "I present to you, Dr. Natalie Scott."

CHAPTER FORTY-TWO
The Kern River
Memorial Day Weekend

Jamie invited Natalie to drive up to the dam with him a day early to beat Memorial Day traffic. Then, he insisted they hike their kayaks down into the ravine below the dam just to check it out. A reconnaissance trip, she thought. That made sense. After all, she was chairwoman of the Friends of the River spring whitewater trip.

When they reached the dry river bed, they gazed downstream and Natalie could imagine what it would be like tomorrow when the authorities let the dam out. Class 7 whitewater rapids? She got a flutter in her heart just thinking of it. It had been a year since she'd been on the river. And what a year!

Then Jamie got a funny look on his face, and gazed up the dam. What was he looking at? In an instant, he gave a military salute to the guard in the station high on the dam's giant fortress.

Natalie thought she saw someone salute back just as water began to spurt from the great wall.

She saw the early sun catch the light spray casting a magnificent rainbow into the morning sky.

The spray grew into a torrential stream and whitewater rapids grew before their very eyes and cascaded through the dry ravine, quickly filling the banks of the Kern.

“Ladies first!” he said.

THE END

Look for more adventures of Natalie Scott